Praise for
How to Bake a Sausage Dog

'**Eccentricity** and **zaniness** abound, with more than a suggestion of the sinister ... Translated by Siobhán Parkinson from the German into **sprightly** English, this novel sparkles with **wit** and **inventiveness**.'

The Irish Times

'The narrative is smooth and well-paced, with plenty of **humour** to keep a younger reader engaged ... The language is fluid and crystal clear and, thanks to Parkinson's expertise, it doesn't feel like a translation ... Each chapter is punctuated with one of David Roberts' **visual delights**. His exquisite, hand-executed style matches the text brilliantly, and the result is both **atmospheric** and **soulful**.'   *Inis Magazine*

'Translated by Siobhán Parkinson from the German into **lively** English, this is a **fast-paced** adventure story. **Exquisite** black-and-white line drawings by David Roberts make it especially pleasing.'

The Irish Independent

'A wonderfully **surreal** story that successfully mixes humour with the slightly **gruesome** to create an imaginative romp that carries the reader along ... For confident young readers who enjoy the unusual.'

Books for Keeps

'The translation from German by Siobhán Parkinson captures all the **zany off-beat humour**.'   *Outside In World*

KIRSTEN REINHARDT

How to Bake a Sausage Dog

Illustrated by David Roberts

Translated by Siobhán Parkinson

HOW TO BAKE A SAUSAGE DOG

First published 2011 as
Fennymores Reise oder wie man ein Dackel im Salzmantel macht
by Carlsen Verlag GmBH, Hamburg, Germany
Text and illustrations © Carlsen Verlag 2011
All rights reserved

This translation first published in 2014 as *Fennymore and the Brumella or
How to Salt-bake a Dachshund* by Little Island Books

This edition first published in 2019 by
Little Island Books
7 Kenilworth Park
Dublin 6W
Ireland

Translation © Siobhán Parkinson 2014

Print ISBN: 978-1-910411-88-9
Ebook (Kindle) ISBN: 978-1-910411-89-6
Ebook (other platforms) ISBN: 978-1-910411-90-2

A British Library Cataloguing in Publication record for this book is available
from the British Library.

Typeset by Catherine Gaffney
Proofread by Emma Dunne
Printed in Poland by Drukarnia Skleniarz

Little Island has received funding to support this book from the Arts
Council of Ireland/An Chomhairle Ealaíon, and from the Arts Council
of Northern Ireland; the translation was partially funded by the Goethe-
Institut and Ireland Literature Exchange.

10 9 8 7 6 5 4 3 2 1

Chapter 1

In which we are introduced to Fennymore Teabreak, Aunt Elsie and the best recipe for salt-baked sausage dog

Fennymore Teabreak was an unusual boy. He ate liver pâté for breakfast, a home-made banana-split for lunch and in the evening he chomped on large celery sticks. If his calculations were correct, he'd be eleven this summer, but he couldn't be sure because he'd never had a birthday party. That had been Aunt Elsie's decision because on Fennymore's eighth birthday his parents had disappeared. They'd never reappeared, and no way did Aunt Elsie want to be reminded of that day. So Fennymore had to work out for himself how old he was and he really couldn't be sure.

Fennymore had tousled brown hair. His right ear was glued to his head like a limpet to a rock, and his left ear stuck out like the handle of a china teacup. Fennymore was neither tall nor short, neither fat nor thin. His best friend was a sky-blue bicycle that thought it was a horse. It had got a bit rusty and its name was Monbijou. That is French for 'my jewel'.

Fennymore and Monbijou lived in The Bronx, a large old house outside town. The shutters were crooked and the roof was buckled. It used to be a blue house, way back, but all the rain had washed the colour away. It has to be said that Fennymore lived in a rainy kind of area. All the sun had also bleached the colour out because Fennymore also lived in a sunny kind of area. People around there always carried rain hats. When it rained, they put them on their heads, and when it was sunny, they let them dangle on a string around their necks.

Aunt Elsie bought two or three dashing flowery rain hats every week because the rain hats that they had in that area were not very durable. That's why there were so many rain-hat shops in town. Twenty-four, to be precise. Fennymore didn't have the money to be buying rain hats, so he just made his own out of newspaper.

Since his parents had disappeared, Fennymore lived all alone in his big wind-battered house. Well, not quite alone, because luckily Monbijou lived with him in The Bronx. And then, of course, there was Aunt Elsie.

Aunt Elsie lived in town, right over the Tristesse Ice-Cream Parlour, and she visited Fennymore every Sunday at exactly three minutes past three. Every Sunday they ate salt-baked sausage dog and drank elderflower tea. Anyone who has prepared salt-baked sausage dog knows what a lengthy and complicated business it is. It takes a lot of patience and a lot of skill. First you have to find a suitable sausage dog. It must be not too fat but not too lean either. It has to be just right, a perfect edible sausage dog.

Aunt Elsie's favourite hunting ground for sausage dogs was the city centre because that was where the local pensioners went strolling all day long with their sausage dogs, viewing the window displays in the rain-hat shops. Aunt Elsie would spend every Wednesday afternoon eating coffee sundaes in the Tristesse Ice-Cream Parlour. She kept a sharp eye out, under cover of large dark sunglasses, and when a pensioner strolled by with his sausage dog, she shot out of her chair like a whirlwind and crept along behind them. Aunt Elsie was astonishingly agile, considering her age and her full figure. 'Full figure' means that she was dreadfully fat but didn't like anyone to mention it.

The pensioners usually called in to the butcher's to ask for scraps of meat for their dogs. They tied up their darlings outside the door while they went inside. Luckily for Aunt Elsie, sausage dogs were not allowed in the butcher's. Like lightning, she untied the waiting sausage dog, clamped it under her arm as if it were a handbag with paws and scooted off home. And by the time the pensioner came merrily out of the butcher's with his scraps, his pet was well on its way to becoming salt-baked sausage dog.

Sadly, Fennymore could not sit around in the ice-cream parlour eating coffee sundaes. His teacher, Herr Muckenthaler, had spotted him there one time with Aunt Elsie when Fennymore really should have been in maths class. That was very embarrassing for Aunt Elsie because she had encouraged him to skive off. So from then on Fennymore had to hide between the recycling bins in a side street near the ice-cream parlour while Aunt Elsie was eating coffee sundaes.

When Fennymore spotted a sausage dog, he whistled through his fingers. That was the signal for Aunt Elsie.

And that is how Aunt Elsie managed to provide herself with her favourite dish every week. Fenny-more didn't think anything of it. It was all he knew, apart

from pâté, banana-splits and the celery that grew in the garden of The Bronx.

Every week in Fennymore Teabreak's life had been the same since his parents' disappearance. Every Sunday, Aunt Elsie came round and together they ate salt-baked sausage dog and drank elder-flower tea. On Mondays and Tuesdays, Fennymore had tummy ache, and on these days he didn't eat pâté or banana-split, just munched unenthusiastic-ally on a celery stick.

Wednesday was sausage-dog-hunting day, and he would stay overnight with Aunt Elsie so that he could help with the preparation of the salt-baked sausage dog on Thursday morning.

On Fridays, Fennymore bought liver pâté and the ingredients for banana-split.

On Saturdays, Fennymore climbed up onto the roof of The Bronx to view the rainbows of the area. That always made him think of his parents.

His father, Fenibald Teabreak, was an inven-tor and his mother, Regina Teabreak, was really a mathematician, but when she met Fennymore's father, she discovered that she much preferred thinking up inventions to solving mathematical problems. And that is how Fennymore's parents got to be an inventing team. Fennymore's mother drew up the plans and Fennymore's father built the inventions. Fennymore's mother liked to work on the kitchen table in The Bronx, and his father liked to work in the Invention Capsule. The Invention Capsule was a tiny shed overgrown with vines right at the bottom of the garden, behind the currant and gooseberry bushes and the compost heap.

Most of Fennymore's parents' inventions were commissions for other people, but sometimes they invented something for themselves. Fennymore liked the Mechanical Waiter. That's what the toast-popper that his parents had invented was called. This contraption catapulted toast out of the toaster right onto the plate, by means of a chrome spring. Unfortunately the thing broke shortly after Fennymore's parents disappeared and Fennymore had no idea how to repair it, so after that he stopped having toast for breakfast.

The invention that his parents were working on before they disappeared was a great secret. Not even Fennymore was allowed to know anything about it.

These were the things Fennymore thought about when he sat on the roof of The Bronx on Saturdays. And then it was Sunday again, and

Recipe for Salt-Baked Sausage Dog

Ingredients
1 edible sausage dog, medium
3 kilos salt
1 bucket fresh mud

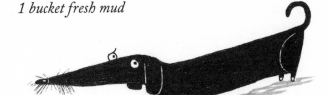

Rub three kilos of salt into the sausage dog, and then cover with enough mud to double its volume. Then allow the prepared sausage dog to rest for fifty-five hours in a cool place, such as a cellar or a larder, to allow the full flavour to develop.

Preheat the oven and bake the sausage dog at a low heat for twelve hours. Allow to cool, and then carefully knock away the mud and salt coating, which, conveniently enough, also removes the sausage dog's hair.

Slice the sausage dog and serve.

Enjoy!

Aunt Elsie came to visit him with the baked sausage dog.

Fennymore had hardly any time to go to school, except on Saturdays, but then the school was closed. After all, Herr Muckenthaler, the teacher, had to get an occasional break. And so it went, week after week, month after month, year after year.

Chapter 2

*In which the story starts because
Aunt Elsie is late*

The day on which the story begins is a Sunday in August, almost three years after the disappearance of Fennymore's parents. Fennymore had just watered the herbs in the living room, had prepared Monbijou's lunch and was waiting for Aunt Elsie.

Aunt Elsie did not come. Normally she was very keen on punctuality and turned up at The Bronx at exactly three minutes past three, lurching and wheezing through the front door, loudly calling, 'Fennymore! Dinner!'

Fennymore was rather surprised when Aunt Elsie had not come lumbering through the door by four minutes past three. By seven minutes past three, when 'Fennymore! Dinner!' had not echoed through the house, he started to worry.

'I'm sorry, Monbijou,' he said to his bicycle, which was standing in the middle of the heap of hay that he had put out for it, 'but I'm afraid you'll have to eat that up later. We have to find out where Aunt Elsie is.'

Monbijou gave an indignant snort. He was feeling hard done by because he always had to eat in the kitchen when Aunt Elsie came visiting. Normally he ate in the living room, but Aunt Elsie thought a bicycle eating hay was ridiculous and didn't want to have to watch.

Fennymore didn't let Monbijou's snorting bother him. He grabbed his newspaper hat and pushed his bicycle outside. It had just stopped raining. The air was steamy and the ground was still soft. Tiny rainbows hung between the celery plants, but Fennymore scarcely noticed them. First he cycled once around The Bronx. Maybe Aunt Elsie was somewhere in the garden. But no, nothing. Coming around to the front door again, Fennymore stuck his head in and called, 'Aunt Elsie?'

When he didn't get an answer, he called a little more loudly, 'Salt-baked sausage dog?'

That was kind of pointless because even if there had been a salt-baked sausage dog in The Bronx it wouldn't have been able to answer. But it was eleven minutes past three and Fennymore was in a bit of a state.

Monbijou braked hard. He always did that when things weren't going his way. Fennymore was feeling a bit antsy himself. He had never gone to town on a Sunday before.

What'll I do if the town isn't there on Sundays? Fennymore thought to himself. It was there on Wednesdays, he knew, because he cycled there on Monbijou to help with the sausage dog hunt. And on Thursdays, when he cycled home after helping to prepare the salt-baked sausage dog, it was also there. And it was there on Fridays when he went shopping. But on Sundays?

Monbijou gave a doubtful snuffle. He really didn't feel like moving.

But Fennymore Teabreak was an inquisitive boy. *If I don't find out, I'll never know*, he said to himself. Deftly, he disconnected Monbijou's brakes, a trick his father had taught him, and off they went.

It was dry and sunny again. Fennymore could see the path stretching out in front of him, so at least that was there on Sundays, as far as he could see. At first they followed the little dirt track edged with sunflowers. Then they turned onto a country laneway where wildflowers and weeds grew on either side. And finally, by a stand of apple trees, they reached the main road, which had a white line down the middle and only a ditch along the side.

Not much was happening on the road. Monbijou gave a disgusted snort every few metres, and Fennymore sang 'We were approaching Madagascar' to him at the top of his voice to cheer him up. That was his favourite song. Also, he had stuffed a handful of hay in his pocket, and he offered Monbijou a few wisps of it whenever he slowed down.

After half an hour, they had reached the outskirts of town. So the town was there on Sundays too. The shopping street with the twenty-four rain-hat shops was there, the butcher's shop, and even the Tristesse Ice-Cream Parlour, outside of which sat ten or eleven pensioners with their sausage dogs, eating coffee sundaes.

So many sausage dogs! thought Fennymore. *I must immediately inform Aunt Elsie.*

Chapter 3

In which a silvery grey gentleman materialises
and everybody speaks at once

Two men and an old lady were talking excitedly at each other outside the door to Aunt Elsie's building, waving their arms about in the air. The old lady was Aunt Elsie's neighbour. She owned a white sausage dog and she always carried it around in her arms. Fennymore wondered if maybe she knew what Aunt Elsie's favourite food was.

Herr Muckenthaler, Fennymore's teacher, was also there and an old man with a large white moustache and a black coat, carrying a black suitcase. In the other hand he had a lead with a fat orange-striped cat on the other end of it. This was Dr Hourgood. Fennymore had visited his surgery a long time ago because he'd had tonsillitis. He'd been very small at the time, and

Dr Hourgood had given him a horrible-tasting medicine. But what were Frau Plüsch, Herr Muckenthaler and Dr Hourgood doing standing outside Aunt Elsie's apartment block? And where was Aunt Elsie? It all seemed very odd to Fennymore.

Suddenly a man appeared in the doorway. He came out of nowhere, you might say.

Fennymore immediately got the hiccups. That always happened when something unusual and exciting was going on. The last time it happened was the time Aunt Elsie had accidentally prepared salt-baked sausage dog with sugar instead of salt.

The curious gentleman who was the cause of Fennymore's hiccups this time was unbelievably tall and thin, so tall and thin, in fact, that it looked as if he might snap in the middle at any moment. His old-fashioned clothes – he wore a morning coat with tails and a bowtie – were all silvery grey. Even his hair and his face seemed to be silvery grey, just like his large thin hands. In one of these silvery grey hands he held a long silvery grey wand, and at the tip of this wand was a bright light.

The silvery grey gentleman stood for a moment beside Frau Plüsch, Herr Muckenthaler and Dr

Hourgood, though they didn't seem to notice him at all. They were still waving their arms around and talking over each other. Only the fat cat hissed and arched its back, which made it look even fatter. Dr Hourgood jerked impatiently on the lead.

This silvery grey gentleman looks familiar somehow, thought Fennymore, though he couldn't remember if they had ever met. The man's face looked awfully old and wrinkly, but somehow not unkind. For a moment, they caught each other's eye. The silvery grey man stretched his eyes in surprise, and Fennymore felt a chill running down his back, as if someone had stuck a scoop of vanilla ice-cream down his collar. He gave a particularly loud hiccup. And suddenly the silvery grey man disappeared.

But Frau Plüsch, Herr Muckenthaler and Dr Hourgood had spotted Fennymore on the opposite side of the street and came running towards him, all of a flap.

'My poor, poor boy,' wailed Frau Plüsch, tears running down her face.

She dug her pointy little fingers into his arm and the white sausage dog in her arms began to lick his ear. Fennymore pulled a face and hiccupped.

Herr Muckenthaler spoke sharply. 'Frau Plüsch, I must ask you to take that dog away. You must see that Fennymore is quite overcome.'

Indeed Fennymore Teabreak was rather overcome. And so he was very glad when Dr Hourgood cleared his throat and Frau Plüsch and Herr Muckenthaler fell silent and looked respectfully at the doctor.

'Hmmm,' went Dr Hourgood. 'Dear Fennymore Teabreak ...'

But he said no more. He just looked thoughtfully at the gleaming toes of his polished shoes.

'Yes?' said Fennymore and hiccupped. He gave an embarrassed grin.

Dr Hourgood drew his bushy eyebrows together in a frown and regarded Fennymore suspiciously.

'Hmmm,' went Dr Hourgood again. 'Dear Fennymore Teabreak, I have to inform you that your great-aunt, Elisabeth Grosskornschroth, has gone from us.'

Fennymore was not quite sure if he had properly understood what Dr Hourgood had said. Elisabeth Grosskornschroth was Aunt Elsie. That was her full name. And 'gone from us' meant that she had died. Stone dead. Kicked the bucket.

'I – Aunt Elsie – *hic* – is dead?' Fennymore asked. 'That – *hic* – can't be true,' he added quietly.

But it could be true. That was clear to Fennymore when he looked into the mortified faces of the adults.

Suddenly he felt quite lost and dreadfully small. He gulped.

Frau Plüsch gave a heartrending sob. 'Oh, the poor boy!'

Dr Hourgood gave a thoughtful frown. His big white moustache trembled a little.

'So, well then, um, hmm,' he said. 'My dear Fennymore Teabreak, I must ask you, in view of the situation, to sign the death certificate of the late lamented Elisabeth Grosskornschroth, for the record.'

Dr Hourgood handed Fennymore a parchment scroll and took a large old fountain pen out of his coat pocket. Since Fennymore hardly ever went to school, he couldn't read all that very well, but of course he could write his name. He inscribed *Fennymore Teabreak* artistically in the place that Dr Hourgood pointed to with his fat finger, using Dr Hourgood's big old fountain pen.

No sooner had Fennymore finished than the doctor rolled up the parchment, said, 'Hmm,' again, 'good,' gave his eyebrows a thoughtful wiggle and took his leave. Fennymore watched him go and hiccupped.

Chapter 4

In which there is tea with honey cookies and Fennymore sits in an outlandishly decorated living room

No sooner had the doctor disappeared than Frau Plüsch's white sausage dog started trying to lick Fennymore again.

'Frau Plüsch, I think you'd better go indoors,' said Herr Muckenthaler crossly. It was pretty clear that he wanted to get rid of the old lady along with her dog.

Fennymore had had enough of all this nonsense.

'Could somebody here please tell me what has actually happened?' he yelled so loudly that the pensioners across the road in the ice-cream parlour nearly dropped their false teeth into their sundaes.

And so loudly that his hiccups disappeared.

Frau Plüsch and Herr Muckenthaler gazed in astonishment at Fennymore Teabreak, as if they had forgotten that he was there. Then Herr Muckenthaler put an arm around Fennymore and looked ingratiatingly at Frau Plüsch and her ridiculous dog.

'Frau Plüsch,' he said, 'I think we could all do with a cup of tea.'

When Fennymore entered Frau Plüsch's house, he almost got dizzy – it was so overstuffed and brightly coloured. The carpet was so riotously patterned that he was dazzled by it, and the walls were covered with gold-framed photographs of Paula, the white sausage dog. Fennymore and Herr Muckenthaler stood awkwardly in the hallway, peering into the living room, almost every square inch of which was adorned with lace doilies.

Frau Plüsch seemed not to notice how awkward they felt and waved them through the door.

'Take a seat there on the sofa,' she said brightly, 'while I put the kettle on for a nice cup of tea.'

Fennymore and Herr Muckenthaler looked at each other and sank into the soft sofa together. Fennymore had sat in his mucky trousers on a piece of white lace. He pulled it from under him and spread it out with his hands, which were not much cleaner. Where to put it?

He looked sideways at his teacher, who was staring at one of the sausage dog portraits. He was wearing, as usual, a light-brown corduroy suit. He had put his battered leather briefcase beside him on the carpet. He was the school's youngest teacher and the only one who had not yet given up trying to convince Fennymore of the necessity of education. The other teachers had copped on long ago.

He's really very nice, Fennymore thought to himself, with a sudden pang of conscience.

While Frau Plüsch was pottering around in the kitchen, Fennymore fiddled with the lace doily and looked more closely at the sausage dog portraits. The big green eyes of Frau Plüsch's white sausage dog looked out of every single gold frame. The same colour as my mother's eyes, Fennymore thought. He liked thinking about her, but somehow he had got used to life with Monbijou, Aunt Elsie and salt-baked sausage dog – it was all that he had left – and now it seemed as if even that was about to come to an end.

Frau Plüsch came out of the kitchen, carrying a small silver tray. Paula, the white sausage dog, came trotting behind her. Frau Plüsch handed around china cups of nettle tea.

'You'll be hungry after that shock you got, you poor boy,' she said, pushing a plate of biscuits towards him.

Her worried tone was getting on Fennymore's nerves. Herr Muckenthaler cast an envious glance at the biscuits and cleared his throat.

'Many thanks, Frau Plüsch,' he said. 'And as for you, Fennymore. You'll be wanting to know what your great-aunt died of?'

Fennymore nodded. Actually, he wasn't at all sure that he wanted to know, but Herr Muckenthaler's question didn't really sound like a question at all. Without taking any notice of Fennymore's nod, Herr Muckenthaler went on talking.

'Well, son, she died of sausage dog poisoning.'

Herr Muckenthaler threw Frau Plüsch an apologetic look. She paled and dug her fingers into the hair of the sausage dog that had made itself comfortable on her lap. Paula yowled.

'We think,' said Herr Muckenthaler nervously, 'that you are old enough to hear this. It seems that your great-aunt lived mostly on sausage dog.'

Fennymore almost laughed out loud because that was not exactly news to him. He was just about to tell Herr Muckenthaler this, but looking at Frau Plüsch and her sausage dog, he decided that Aunt Elsie's Sunday visits with salt-baked sausage dog were best kept to himself. Frau Plüsch had gone green, and the little sausage dog was whimpering anxiously.

At that very moment, Fennymore's tummy started to rumble. No wonder, because under normal circumstances he would by now have devoured a good quarter of Aunt Elsie's speciality. He put the lace cloth down on the table and took a honey cookie. He bit into it experimentally. He'd completely forgotten how good cookies were. Three – no, seven, no, twenty-four – times as good as salt-baked sausage dog.

Drooling, Herr Muckenthaler watched Fennymore with a mixture of envy and sympathy.

'Your great-aunt was apparently in the habit of eating a sausage dog a week. But, although she prepared a – um – fresh sausage dog each week' – Herr Muckenthaler spoke the word 'fresh' with an

anxious sidelong glance at Frau Plüsch and Paula –
'it would appear that she also ate up the leftover
sausage dog from her larder, even if it had already
started to go mouldy.'

Fennymore imagined Aunt Elsie sneaking into
the larder at night in her enormous flowery night-
dress and gobbling up the remains of last week's
sausage dog.

'Urgh!' went Fennymore.

A biscuit crumb had got stuck in his throat,
but Herr Muckenthaler and Frau Plüsch inter-
preted his 'Urgh' as an indication of how revolted
he was by Aunt Elsie's eating habits.

'You poor boy,' Frau Plüsch said again.

The white sausage dog licked Fennymore's
fingers gently with its warm, rough tongue. It
tickled and made him laugh. Frau Plüsch gave her
sausage dog an appreciative look and gave Fennymore a smile.

'Now, my dears,' she said, 'it is time for my
afternoon nap. Here, son, get a few more of those
biscuits into you. Herr Muckenthaler, please take
the keys to Elsie's flat and you and Fennymore
go and rescue the valuables before that worthless
crew comes nosing round.'

Chapter 5

In which Fennymore discovers what a worthless crew is and what an orphaned flat feels like

Aunt Elsie's flat smelt just as musty as ever, but it was quiet and weirdly empty. The kitchen clock ticked softly. The fridge hummed. Had it not been for the open door to the kitchen and the yawning emptiness in there, you might have thought nothing had changed, but the wretched remains of the sausage dog in tinfoil had disappeared out of the larder and Aunt Elsie had disappeared too.

Herr Muckenthaler sat down on a kitchen chair. Fennymore found it strange to see his teacher here. Herr Muckenthaler didn't seem all that comfortable either and fiddled around with the lapels of his cord jacket.

'What exactly is a worthless crew?' Fennymore asked into the oppressive silence.

'Worthless crew? Well, *crew* is a nautical term, of course,' his teacher explained, looking gratefully at him. He was in his element. He explained that a crew means the sailors who sail a ship, but that it can also mean any kind of a crowd or group or team of people. And somehow it is not very complimentary, especially not if you add the word *worthless* to it. Fennymore said nothing, but he was impressed.

'Right, Fennymore, choose the things you'd like to keep for yourself. Anything valuable and anything you'd like to remember your great-aunt by. The mayor has already earmarked the flat for a family with seven children, the Kobaldinis. Maybe you know them? Fizzy Kobaldini is in your class.'

Fennymore felt dreadfully ashamed about all the bunking off school he did.

'Sure. She's the one with the freckles,' he said, to show that he did go to school often enough to know Fizzy Kobaldini.

'Exactly,' said Herr Muckenthaler. 'Up to now, the Kobaldinis have been living in the supermarket warehouse and they are delighted to have finally got their own place.'

Fennymore had a think. What should he take from Aunt Elsie's flat? He had everything he needed in The Bronx.

He went to the bathroom and got the little sponge that Aunt Elsie had bought specially for him, so that he could have a bath at her place after helping to prepare the salt-baked sausage dog. In the bedroom, he opened Aunt Elsie's big wardrobe and was quite dazzled by the gaudy floral patterns on Aunt Elsie's nightdresses. He closed the wardrobe quickly. In the kitchen, he felt under the potatoes that were in a crate behind the stove pipe and pulled out a vinegar-chocolate tin in which, he knew, Aunt Elsie kept her prize possessions.

So that was that.

Fennymore wedged the chocolate tin under his arm, stuffed the sponge in his pocket and took a last look around the flat. His eye fell on a flowery rain hat hanging on the wardrobe door. It was quite new. He made a snap decision. He took off his own battered newspaper hat, put it on top of the wardrobe and hung Aunt Elsie's rain hat around his neck instead.

It was raining as Fennymore stepped out onto the street with Herr Muckenthaler. He put Aunt Elsie's rain hat on his head. Herr Muckenthaler also pulled on his own rain hat, one with a corduroy pattern.

'Shall I drive you home?' he asked.

'No thanks,' Fennymore answered. 'I've got my horse.'

Herr Muckenthaler gave him an astonished look, but then he shook his head and said, 'Well, Fennymore, as perhaps you know, the summer holidays have started. That means no school for six weeks. Though in your case that's hardly ... well, anyway, I'd be delighted to see you in my class at the beginning of the next school year. Regularly. It would be good for you to spend time with other children.' Herr Muckenthaler sounded kind but firm. 'And if you feel lonely over the next few weeks and would like someone to talk to, you are very welcome to come and see me. This is my address.'

With these words he handed Fennymore a piece of paper, which Fennymore quickly stuck in his pocket along with the sponge, so his teacher wouldn't see that he couldn't read it. 'Thank you,' he said.

Herr Muckenthaler shook Fennymore's hand, looked at him with a concerned expression, gave him a friendly slap on the shoulder and said, 'Well then, Fennymore. You know, you really shouldn't take what Frau Plüsch said to heart. The Kobaldinis are not a worthless crew. They're just a family like any other.'

With that, he set off.

Now Fennymore was all alone. He looked up, through the raindrops, at the front of the house where Aunt Elsie had lived. The windows of her flat were dark. The pensioners had left the Tristesse Ice-Cream Parlour and the empty street looked miserable. Fennymore pulled his flowery rain hat down over his face and shuffled his way to the other side of the street to get Monbijou. All he wanted to do now was go home and eat a banana-split in The Bronx and reflect quietly on what had happened that Sunday.

But Monbijou wasn't there. There wasn't a sign of a sky-blue bicycle anywhere. Fennymore looked up and down both sides of the street. Not so much as a glimpse of a carrier or a glimmer of sky blue was to be seen. Perhaps Monbijou had gone home on his own?

It came back to Fennymore that he had let go of his bike at just the same moment as the silvery grey gentleman had materialised in Aunt Elsie's doorway. If that weird fellow brought on my hiccups, he thought, Monbijou could easily have cycled off from sheer shock. And so he set off on the path to The Bronx.

Chapter 6

*In which Fennymore walks alone
through the dark grey night*

Fennymore's head was in turmoil. Lost in thought, he dawdled along past the twenty-four rain-hat shops and the butcher's shop. The rain was easing off and dusk was falling.

A rustling in his jacket pocket reminded Fennymore about the bag of honey cookies that Frau Plüsch had given him to take home. Fennymore pulled the bag out of his pocket and took out one of the golden brown biscuits. As soon as he bit into it, the sweet taste of honey gave him renewed strength.

By now he'd walked a good way along the street and could make out the stand of apple trees behind which was the path to The Bronx. The trees stretched their branches up against the now greyish sky.

In the area where Fennymore lived, it never got really pitch dark. The night was more a kind of dark grey. Fennymore knew why, because it was in the *Dictionary of Inventions*.

The *Dictionary of Inventions* was an old notebook in which Fennymore's parents noted their ideas for new inventions, but for Fennymore it had become, over time, a kind of source of enlightenment. In the past, when his mother and father had lived with him in The Bronx, they had often read bits out of it as a bedtime story, and that was how Fennymore knew a lot of stuff, even though he seldom went to school. He knew the definitions given in the *Dictionary of Inventions* off by heart. Sometimes he rehearsed them quietly to himself. And so it was that he walked through the dark grey night, whispering:

Dark grey night, The: *The night in this area is dark grey, not to be confused with the usual pitch-dark night. The large number (countless) of stars above us mixes in a particular way with the residual damp of the raindrops that can be detected at night on the foliage and grass. The interplay of starlight and raindrops produces a refraction of light that is hardly perceptible to the naked eye but that, through a multiplication effect, leads to the phenomenon of the dark grey night.*

Fennymore wasn't
afraid as he walked
home to The Bronx
all alone. He was lost
in thoughts about his
parents' *Dictionary of
Inventions* and took
no notice of where
he was going. And so
he had no notion that
two ice-green-grey eyes
were watching him out
of the apple trees. Nor did
he notice that a very tall thin
gentleman in a morning coat
was hiding among the branches, frantically trying,
as Fennymore approached, to hide the bright light
at the tip of his long wand with a couple of leaves.
So deep in thought was Fennymore that he didn't
even hear the creaking of the boughs, the sudden
bump and the soft 'Ouch' as the silvery grey gentleman fell out of the tree and landed on the seat
of his pants. It was only when a brightly shining
light came shooting skywards, fizzing, out of the
apple trees that Fennymore was briefly startled.
Though, after all the extraordinary events of that

Sunday, a fizzing light shooting out of an apple tree didn't make all that much of an impression on Fennymore. He retreated immediately into his thoughts again and didn't hear the muffled grumbling and the scurrilous swearing that were pouring out of the thickly grown grass under the apple trees.

Fennymore turned onto the laneway lined with wild flowers and soon came to the dirt track that brought him right up to his own front door. The Bronx was etched blackly against the sky. *All dark*, Fennymore noted sadly and gave a sigh. He'd been hoping that Monbijou would be home before him, would have put on the light and would be quietly eating his hay in the kitchen or having a snooze in the living room.

Fennymore entered the house. He'd only been gone since midday, but it felt as if he'd been away for an eternity, so much had changed in his life in the meantime.

The kitchen door was ajar. Fennymore pushed it open with his foot and put the vinegar-chocolate tin and Aunt Elsie's brightly patterned rain hat on the big well-polished kitchen table. The pile of hay was just as high as it had been when he'd left with Monbijou at eleven minutes past three.

Nothing had changed in the living room either. The herbs were growing away quietly to themselves. Fennymore's father's big leather sofa stood like a grand monument, casting a shadow, in the middle of the room. The little table that Fennymore had cleared especially for Aunt Elsie was bare. Spick and span and no sign of the remains of salt-baked sausage dog that would usually be on it at this time on a Sunday evening. All that was on it were the gold-rimmed china plates, the silver cutlery and the elderflower-tea cups that Fennymore had taken out of the kitchen cupboard that morning. Everything looked exactly as it had when Fennymore had left in the afternoon. Except that Fennymore's sky-blue and normally very trusty steed was nowhere to be seen.

Tired and at a loss, Fennymore slumped onto the sofa, covered himself with the multicoloured blanket that was draped over it and fell asleep.

Chapter 7

*In which Fizzy Kobaldini turns up in
The Bronx, Fennymore does a lot of talking
and a decision gets made*

It was bright when Fennymore woke up. He
scratched his head sleepily. What day was it? Ah,
yes, Monday, tummy-ache day. But Fennymore
didn't have tummy ache. Nor did he feel like celery.
He'd much prefer one of Frau Plüsch's honey
cookies, but unfortunately he'd polished those off
the previous evening.

He got up from the sofa, pulled on his crum-
pled jeans and pressed his left ear against his
head. He did that every morning, in the hope
that it would eventually come to cling to his head
like a limpet to a rock. Fennymore had picked
up this tip from watching the old ladies in the
Tristesse Ice-Cream Parlour. They were always
hitting themselves under the chin with the backs

of their hands. Aunt Elsie had explained that they believed that helped to get rid of their double chins.

After he had pressed his ear against his head and it had immediately sprung back into its original position, Fennymore looked up. Fizzy Kobaldini was standing in the doorway.

That it was Fizzy Kobaldini was beyond doubt. A shaggy ponytail, a face full of freckles and wearing over-washed, mousy brown boys' clothes. All the Kobaldini children wore hand-me-downs from Marlon, the eldest, and since Fizzy was the youngest of seven, they looked pretty worn by the time they got to her. She was wearing Fennymore's old rain hat. He recognised it by the picture of the Tristesse Ice-Cream Parlour, which was part of an ad for the new deluxe coffee sundae.

Fennymore went red to the very tip of his sticky-out ear. How long had she been watching him?

'Hey, what do you think you're doing here?' The question came tumbling out all by itself. 'And what are you looking at?'

Fennymore sounded downright unfriendly.

Fizzy gaped at him in surprise.

'Well, I heard what happened,' she said grandly, 'and I thought you might be feeling sad and lonely. Besides, it's the summer holidays, so I can do what I like.'

Sad? Lonely? Him?

He was still half-asleep. The events of yesterday were pretty hazy. But as his head cleared, it all started to come back to him. He didn't want Fizzy to know how he was really feeling, so he did his best to give her a cheery grin.

'Ah, I'm fine,' he said, but it didn't sound very convincing. Fennymore slumped back sheepishly onto the sofa.

'Anyway, I had another reason for coming,' Fizzy said, sinking down beside him on the sofa. 'You've probably heard that we're living in your great-aunt's flat now.'

He certainly had. Fennymore felt like saying something rude, but then he thought better of it. It wasn't Fizzy's fault that Aunt Elsie's flat had been passed along so quickly.

Fizzy gave him a serious look. 'I think it's all a bit odd. But I'm the only one. My parents and my brothers are all too busy being thrilled that we don't have to live in the supermarket warehouse any longer.'

Fizzy was careful not to mention that they were also busy laughing at Marlon, who was prancing around the living room in one of Aunt Elsie's flowery nighties, with a pillow stuffed up it, calling, 'Where's my yummy sausage dog?'

'How come we got a flat all of a sudden, like lightning, within hours of your aunt's death, when my parents have been queuing up every Monday morning at half past six outside the social-housing office, begging to move out of the supermarket warehouse. Every time, they were told, "The ways of bureaucracy are slow and tortuous" or "The flats have been allocated to upright citizens who pay their way". And now all of a sudden we have a flat, but we had to promise the mayor that we would immediately hand up any documents we might find there. In my book, that stinks to high heaven.'

Fennymore found this hard to listen to, and he had absolutely no interest in hearing what stank to high heaven in Fizzy's life. But Fizzy didn't appear to notice his lack of interest.

'Look, there's even been something about it in the paper.' She swept the rain hat off her head and spread it out. 'Sorry, I always read the rain hats. We have no books at home. Look, here.'

She stabbed at the paper with her grubby little index finger. Fennymore gave the letters, which sat like ants on the paper, an embarrassed look.

'So what?' he said, trying to sound as unconcerned as possible. How could there be anything important in this newspaper?

Fizzy rolled her eyes. 'Fennymore, can you by any chance not read?'

Fennymore couldn't read properly, but since Fizzy's question didn't really sound like a question, he decided not to answer it.

Fizzy read aloud, in a clear but disgusted tone: '"And so the mayor, Dr Rufus Hourgood, has announced that socially deprived families are to receive no further assistance, with immediate effect." That shows how very odd it is that we have been allowed to move into your great-aunt's flat. But I'm sorry.' Fizzy interrupted herself and put a hand on his arm. 'I didn't let you say anything at all, I just prattled on myself. That's the way you have to be in my house. Otherwise you'd never get a word in edgeways.'

So then Fizzy stopped talking and Fennymore told her everything that had gone on in the last twenty-four hours. It all came bursting out of him – he didn't know why. Normally Fennymore was not such a chatterbox, but then he'd never had anyone to talk to, or at least nobody of his own age.

Fizzy listened in silence, her eyes getting wider and wider with every word. When Fennymore had finished, she frowned.

'Monbijou has disappeared, you say. Your sky-blue bicycle. So what are you waiting for? Let's go!' she cried adventurously.

Fennymore felt overwhelmed. 'Why? What? Where to?' he asked.

'Where to is a good question,' Fizzy replied. 'But what do you mean, "Why"? Don't you want to find Monbijou?'

That tone of voice again that didn't sound like a question.

'Maybe this weird silvery guy you saw had something to do with his disappearance. In any case, we have to find your bike. That's as clear as day,' Fizzy said briskly.

Fennymore suddenly regretted having trusted her with so much information. She was going to wreak havoc on his life. He longed for a normal

Monday in a normal week. But this week was not going to be normal. That much he knew.

'You're right,' he said. 'But Monbijou could be a long way off by now. He can go very fast when he wants to. And what will your parents say if you disappear just like that?'

'Oh,' said Fizzy, rubbing her hands clean on her trousers, 'they'll never notice. There are so many of us, they lose count. Titus spent two days and nights locked in the supermarket's bean store before they missed him. He farted for three weeks after. Anyway, they're so busy being delighted about the new flat that they have no interest in anything else. Except for Marlon, who –'

Fizzy stopped herself suddenly. She'd almost let it slip that they were all busy laughing at Marlon prancing about in Aunt Elsie's flowery nighties, calling, 'Where is my yummy sausage dog?'

Fennymore went into the kitchen and packed four celery stalks, two lots of liver pâté and three bananas into his blue gym-bag as provisions for the journey. Then he grabbed a handful of hay and he went back to Fizzy in the living room. She stared in astonishment at the hay.

'Monbijou will be hungry when we find him,' he explained and went a bit red.

Fizzy looked at him as if he had announced that vinegar chocolates were his staple diet. 'Monbijou is a bicycle,' she said. 'How can a bicycle eat hay?'

'It's just that he thinks he's a horse. I have no idea why.'

Fennymore really didn't know. As far back as he could remember, Monbijou had been his horse.

Chapter 8

*In which Fennymore and Fizzy set off
into the wide blue yonder*

'Which direction should we go in? Should we
toss a coin?' Fizzy was standing indecisively at
the garden gate, looking along the dirt track.
To the left it wound its way to the laneway and
to the right it came to a sudden halt at a stone
wall. Fennymore was just about to close the front
door behind him when he remembered Aunt
Elsie's chocolate tin and he went back into the
kitchen.

The tin was still on the kitchen table, where it
had stood quietly all night. He had this feeling that
he shouldn't just leave it lying around. Aunt Elsie
must have had a reason for hiding it under the
potatoes. But where should he put it? He wrapped
the tin in an old tea-towel. Then he looked around

the kitchen. There was the big wooden table where his mother used to draw up her invention plans, the three wobbly chairs, the old kitchen cabinet, in which was a whole collection of cups and plates and where Fennymore kept his provisions, the gas stove and the sink in which last week's dirty dishes were piled up. There weren't many hiding places. Then his eyes fell on the big rubbish bin. Nobody would ever think of looking there for Aunt Elsie's most precious things.

Fennymore lifted the lid. It contained a couple of banana skins, an empty ice-cream tub and the squashed packet of an old liver pâté. It didn't smell exactly appetising. *A perfect hiding place*, Fennymore thought happily and pushed the box under the rubbish. He wiped his hands on his jeans and ran outside.

Fizzy was leaning against the gatepost. 'Right or left, left or right?' she murmured.

Fennymore's gaze fell on the dry-stone wall. Tiny rainbows glittered between the mossy flowers.

Hadn't Monbijou often stood on this very spot looking out over the wall? His bicycle had never much liked cycling to town. If his bike had really taken to its heels to give the silvery gentleman the slip, as Fennymore supposed he had, then he would definitely have gone in this direction.

'The wide blue yonder starts on the other side of the wall behind the house,' Aunt Elsie had always said, 'and you have no business going there.'

But he didn't care about that now. They had to go into the wide blue yonder to find Monbijou.

Fennymore took a deep breath to give himself courage. Then he began to climb onto the little stone wall. It wasn't very high, but the area in which Fennymore lived was so flat that the view from the top of it was wonderful all the same. To the left he could see the houses at the edge of town. The Bronx stood, a washed-out blue against the sky, not far behind him. The crooked shutters were open and Fennymore could make out, on the other side of the window, the outline of the kitchen cabinet. He thought wistfully of the safe and cosy sofa with its comfy blanket in the living room.

Comfy blanket, The: *The Teabreak family's comfy blanket is an essential object in the Bronx household. It has to remain on the large leather sofa at all times. It is made of soft wool and its multicoloured tartan pattern hinders the visibility of the stains that the careless consumption of red wine, coffee and hot chocolate would otherwise leave on it. Its smell is crucial. Only the regular use of the blanket by various members of the family produces this delicious aroma: the smell of security. And because of this particular circumstance, the comfy blanket may never be washed.*

'I beg your pardon?' A freckled face shoved itself under Fennymore's nose and two blue eyes regarded him curiously. 'What circumstances exactly must never be washed?'

Fennymore was shocked into silence. He hadn't been aware that he'd been muttering to himself. 'Em, I just meant …' Fennymore stuttered. 'Well, what I meant to say was … I think we should go this way.'

He stretched out his arm into the wide blue yonder. By now they were standing side by side on top of the wall, fields stretching before them out as far as the horizon. A long way off they could see hills and a little bit of woodland.

'Looks good to me,' Fizzy cried with a whoop and hopped down onto the other side of the wall.

Fennymore took one last look round. An enormous rainbow hung over the roof of The Bronx. Then he also hopped down onto the grass on the other side of the wall.

***

Fennymore and Fizzy made their way, chatting, through the poppies and cornflowers that grew along the edge of the field. That is to say, Fizzy chatted to Fennymore. She told him all about her family. How her father, a fitter, had lost his job some years ago when Dr Hourgood had made the town the capital of the rain-hat industry and metal workers were no longer needed. She told him how the whole Kobaldini family had moved into the supermarket warehouse and how they had made beds for themselves out of large cardboard boxes. And she told him how her six brothers sometimes got on her nerves.

Fennymore found it all very interesting. He was amazed at what Fizzy told him about what they ate. On Sundays the Kobaldini family ate thick pancakes and sometimes there was fizzy lemonade too if the supermarket manager had given them a few out-of-date bottles.

All of a sudden, he became dreadfully embarrassed about his eating habits, and in particular the contents of his gym-bag. Celery, liver pâté and unsplit bananas – who on earth ate things like that? Obviously not Fizzy.

Although I haven't told her that on Sundays I always ate salt-baked sausage dog, Fennymore thought with relief.

'Let's take a break.' Fizzy's voice interrupted his musings. It was starting to drizzle and they had stopped at an enormous haystack. 'I can't go another step and I'm hungry.'

She made a lunge for the gym-bag that hung from his shoulder.

Horrified, Fennymore held his breath. If Fizzy unpacked his lunch, she'd finally realise what a weirdo he was.

But Fizzy had snuggled in among the hay and was already examining the contents of his gym-bag. She took everything out, one by one.

'Let's see. Celery. Hmm. Pâté. Aha. Bananas. Good. And the hay. Interesting selection. But there's plenty of hay here already,' she joked and plumped for a banana.

It was as if a weight lifted from Fennymore's shoulders. It occurred to him how hungry he was too. He squirmed in beside Fizzy in the little hay-cave and bit with a joyful crunch into the celery.

He squinched up his eyes to see if he could make out The Bronx in the distance. Not a thing to be seen. He couldn't even see the tallest building in town. They'd come a long way!

'So what's the story with your parents?' Fizzy asked, giving him a curious sideways look.

'Yeah, well,' said Fennymore and hung his head. He said nothing for a while. But then he told Fizzy as much as he knew.

That his parents had disappeared about three years ago. That from that day to this, he had lived all alone in The Bronx and that Aunt Elsie had looked after him. That his birthday had become a forgotten day. It did him good to get it off his chest.

When Fennymore had stopped speaking and was just trying to decide if he should let Fizzy into the salt-baked sausage-dog story, he realised that she had fallen asleep. The sun was still high in the sky and the hay tickled his chin. Fennymore felt sleepy too. He pulled Aunt Elsie's flowery rain hat down over his eyes and nodded off.

Chapter 9

In which Fennymore and Fizzy find Monbijou and fetch up in a weird kind of place

Ting-a-ling! Fennymore was dreaming about a sky-blue bicycle. It was using a string of liver-pâté sausages as a tightrope that was stretched between two high-rise buildings and it was ringing its bell. *Ting-a-ling!* The tinkling was getting louder, the sausages were swaying dangerously and – no! – the bicycle tottered and fell, fell, fell into the depths. Fennymore jerked awake and opened his eyes.

The sun was lower in the sky and something was sticking into his back. Fennymore pulled a handful of hay out of his shirt and in doing so he touched something soft.

'Hrmph,' muttered Fizzy in her sleep.

Then Fennymore heard it again. *Ting-a-ling.* This time the sound was softer than in his dream.

Muffled, somehow. Fennymore pulled himself together, sat up and pressed his left ear against his head. The ringing sound seemed to come from behind him.

Slowly, he crept around the piled-up hay. Now Fennymore could hear a chomping sound. He poked his head carefully around the corner of the haystack and what he saw brought on the hiccups again. Monbijou was up to his pedals in hay, munching away.

'Mon – *hic* – bijou!' Fennymore cried out loud.

All at once, his bicycle came leaping backwards out of the haystack, shook hay off himself and gave Fennymore a delighted poke with his handlebars. Fennymore was so thrilled to see Monbijou that he forgot he was angry with him. After all, Fennymore had abandoned him outside the Tristesse Ice-Cream Parlour. He swept a few wisps of hay from the saddle of his sky-blue bicycle.

'Monbijou!' he said. 'What a – *hic* – piece of luck! But of course you don't know what has been going on. Aunt Elsie has died and – *hic* –'

But Monbijou interrupted Fennymore's excited chatter and hiccupping with another tinkle.

Fennymore looked up and saw Fizzy coming around the haystack, yawning.

'May I introduce you?' Fennymore said. 'Fizzy Kobaldini, Monbijou. Monbijou, Fizzy Kobaldini.'

Monbijou gave a little bow and Fizzy giggled. 'You're a great bike – eh – horse,' she corrected herself, stroking Monbijou's saddle.

He gave a little leap into the air so that the rest of the hay fell out of his spokes.

Fennymore was so relieved and delighted that he almost forgot that Aunt Elsie had just died and his life was in tatters. Here he was with Fizzy Kobaldini and Monbijou somewhere in the wide blue yonder but he didn't feel at all lonely.

'Well, gentlemen,' said Fizzy. 'Let's get back. I have no intention of staying here overnight. If you have eggs, milk, sugar and flour, I'll make pancakes for us as soon as we get home.'

'Fine,' said Fennymore. 'Sit up there on the carrier and hold on tight because the ground is pretty bumpy here, isn't it, Monbijou?'

He gave his old bicycle a loving look. Monbijou snorted his agreement and let Fennymore and Fizzy climb on.

Fennymore stroked the handlebars and said softly to Fizzy, 'It must be down to you. He's not normally so co-operative.'

Fizzy giggled.

Monbijou waited politely until Fizzy had got a good hold on Fennymore and then he took off. But not towards The Bronx. Monbijou was going in the opposite direction. His wheels turned faster and faster. He jolted heedlessly over stones and stubble in the field so that Fennymore and Fizzy were jostled around and found it difficult to hang on.

'Stop!' Fennymore yelled. 'You're going the wrong way.'

'Slow down!' yelled Fizzy. 'You're going far too fast.'

But Monbijou ignored his flailing, screeching passengers and cycled further and further into the wide blue yonder.

***

It was almost night by the time the crazy journey came to an end. The sky-blue bicycle jerked to a halt. Fizzy was tossed onto the grass with a cry of surprise.

'Ouch!' she shouted. 'Take it easy, Monbijou.'

Fennymore dismounted stiffly, his legs wobbling. He gave Fizzy a hand and helped her to her feet.

'Ouch, my back!' Fizzy groaned, which made Fennymore realise also that every bone in his body hurt.

Monbijou nuzzled and snuffled apologetically in Fennymore's direction.

'Oh, give over,' Fennymore retorted crankily. 'Where on earth are we?'

It was only then that he noticed how dark it was all around them, almost black. This was not the dark grey night he was used to. They really must have come a long way.

'It's a bit spooky around here,' Fizzy whispered.

'Monbijou, what are we doing here?' Fennymore hissed to his bicycle. 'I don't like this place.'

Their eyes gradually adapted to the dark. They were standing under a giant elm tree. The wind tossed the branches so that the leaves rustled and from time to time a twig was torn off and whirled away. A gust of wind tugged at Fizzy's ponytail and made Fennymore's hair more tossed than ever.

Now they could see that behind the elm was a house. It was a very tiny house, more like a hut, made of wood and pretty shabby. The shutters were closed, but a little light showed through a crack.

Monbijou cycled up to the front door and gave three loud rings. The wind suddenly stopped howling and everything went very quiet. A leaf tumbled from the elm tree and landed on the ground with a dry crackle. Fennymore and Fizzy held their breath.

Something was blundering around inside the hut. A chair was being dragged along. Slow steps came shuffling towards the door. A dry cough could be heard through the wooden walls.

And then the door creaked open. The light from the hut lit up the elm tree. The silvery grey man was watching Monbijou angrily from the doorway.

'Impertinent bicycle!' he said crossly. 'What do you want now? I've told you …'

Then his gaze fell on Fennymore. He fell silent and widened his ice-green-grey eyes. And Fennymore got that feeling again, as if someone had stuffed a scoop of vanilla ice-cream down his collar, and the ice-cream was running slowly down his back.

Chapter 10

In which the silvery grey gentleman finally tells the truth, or at least makes a stab at it

Hot steam rose from the misshapen mugs that the silvery grey gentleman had put in front of Fennymore and Fizzy.

'Mmm, chocolate,' said Fizzy happily and immediately began to blow into her cup.

But Fennymore could not take his eyes off their host. After the silvery grey man had got over his initial shock, he'd started trying to get rid of them.

'And kindly take the children with you,' he'd said to Monbijou.

But Monbijou had stood his ground, jammed on his brakes and haughtily rung his bell.

In the end the silvery grey man had given a terribly loud sigh and invited them in, avoiding Fennymore's eyes the whole time. He invited them to take a seat at the little wooden table that stood in the middle of the bare room. A single candle in the middle of the table lit the room dimly. The silvery grey man was making a great show of busyness in the kitchen.

There was a camping stove on top of a pile of orange boxes, and there was a stack of brown cups on a narrow shelf on the wall. They looked as if they had been made by a potter who was all thumbs. Beside them were several tins of drinking chocolate and a battered milk-jug.

The silvery grey man was still wearing his morning coat with tails and his silvery grey tie. The ceiling of the hut was too low for him, so he moved around at a crouch. Fennymore watched his every move. He was reminded of a spider that was caught in a jar and was feeling its way around on little spindly legs.

The way the silvery grey man opened a drinking-chocolate tin with his long fingers and carefully, oh so carefully, sprinkled it onto the milk with a concealed spoon was almost funny. He took great trouble to spill nothing, but as he turned around and unintentionally caught Fennymore's eye, his hand shook so much that he did in fact spill some of the chocolate powder onto the boxes.

Fennymore swallowed a laugh. He felt strangely sorry for the man.

By the time they all had a cup of hot chocolate in front of them and the silvery grey man had wiped away the last of the spilt drinking chocolate, he had nothing more to do. He looked around helplessly, swivelling on his own axis. Fennymore noticed the long silver-grey wand that he'd had outside the Tristesse Ice-Cream Parlour on Sunday leaning against the wall. Only today there was no bright light at the tip. Following Fennymore's gaze, the silvery grey man suddenly looked even more unhappy.

'This is great chocolate,' Fizzy said into the silence. She seemed to be quite unaware of the tense atmosphere. 'Have you been living here long?' she asked the silvery grey gentleman in a friendly voice.

The silvery grey man threw a quick glance in Monbijou's direction. Fennymore's sky-blue bicycle snorted menacingly. He'd made himself comfortable on the wooden floor by the table and was blocking the way to the door. The silvery grey man sighed and sat down with them at the table.

'Well,' he said in a resigned tone. 'It looks as if I have no choice but to tell the truth.'

'You're right there,' Fennymore said, to his own astonishment.

It had just occurred to him where he had seen the silvery grey gentleman before. It was a long time ago. It must have been shortly after his parents disappeared. Fennymore and Monbijou had been sitting outside the house in the sun. At that time, Fennymore believed that his parents would come back any minute now. As the midday sun reached its highest point in the sky, Fennymore had heard a sound behind the little stone wall. Monbijou was uneasy, but Fennymore thought it was his parents coming back. And then, for a split second, Fennymore saw a face peeping over the wall. A very old and friendly silvery grey face.

'What were you doing that time behind the wall?' Fennymore asked.

The silvery grey man looked him right in the eye for the first time. He blinked nervously.

'Well, Fennymore Teabreak,' he said slowly, as if it was the first time he'd spoken that name and wanted to try the words out in his mouth, 'just the same, basically, as I was doing yesterday in the apple tree, only that time you didn't catch sight of me.'

Fennymore gave the silvery grey gentleman an enquiring look, but the man went on talking.

'I just wanted to see you. When I discovered that Fenibald and Regina had a child, I wanted to call the whole thing off, but it was too late.'

Fizzy spat her drinking chocolate back into her cup and cried, 'You know something about Fennymore's parents? That's wonderful! Where are they?'

Fennymore said nothing. His scalp tingled unpleasantly. He'd twigged that what the silvery grey man knew was not that very wonderful at all.

Chapter 11

The silvery grey gentleman's story

'I wasn't well at the time,' began the silvery grey man. He had pushed away his hot-chocolate cup and had folded his long grey fingers on the table top. He regarded his hands thoughtfully. 'I was depressed and tired and I found the work difficult. A new place every day, all the travelling and the sad faces.' He sighed. 'One day, when I had business in your town, I met Dr Hourgood.'

Fennymore noticed that his long grey fingers trembled slightly when he pronounced the name of the doctor.

'There used to be a different doctor in that town. He'd know when he could do no more and it was time for me to get to work. You know how it is, a person has to go when their time has come, and it is my job to help their soul to find its way.'

The silvery grey gentleman raised his head and looked at the wall where his silvery grey wand was leaning.

'But Dr Hourgood was different. He wanted to do a deal with me. It started with a factory owner. "Let's leave him a few days longer," he said. "And we can split the profit that his company will make between us."

'I said no, I didn't need any money. Dr Hourgood gave me a long hard look and said he could see I was not enjoying the best of health. He stuck a thermometer in my mouth and took my pulse. Then he put on a very worried face and shook his head. Right away I felt worse. The doctor prescribed more rest, but I said I had to keep working. Someone like me doesn't get holidays or days off. I am always on duty.'

The silvery grey man paused and gave them a tortured look. 'Please don't judge me. I had no one to turn to.'

But before Fennymore or Fizzy could answer, he went on, his voice getting softer all the time. Fennymore and Fizzy had to lean forward to hear him.

'I can remember it as if it was yesterday. It was a dark and stormy night, just like this one. The elm was creaking outside the house. I had come back from a hard day's work and was just making myself a hot chocolate. My back was killing me and I had never felt so old. Then Dr Hourgood came knocking on my door. I have no idea how he found me. Nobody knows where I live, and nobody had ever come looking for me before. People normally avoid me. You can imagine how confused I was.

'And then the doctor made a suggestion. It was a bad suggestion, but the more I thought about it, the greater seemed the advantages of this deal.' The silvery grey man sighed and hid his face in his large hands. 'It was an unnatural idea. I should never have had anything to do with it.'

'But you did it anyway?' Fennymore interrupted the silvery grey gentleman

'Yes, I did it anyway,' he said, looking at Fennymore seriously out of his ice-green-grey eyes. 'I fetched two people before their time. And for that, I got the unconditional right to work in the old folks' home in the town. Dr Hourgood promised he would never interfere with my work again and my conditions of employment would improve immeasurably if I did him this favour.'

Fennymore and Fizzy stared at the silvery grey gentleman. Fetched two people before their time? Fennymore was hot and cold at the same time.

'These two people weren't by any chance …'

'Regina and Fenibald Teabreak.' The silvery grey man finished Fennymore's sentence in a deathly voice. 'The doctor had assured me that there were no relations and the pair of them were at death's door in any case. It seemed a bit odd, I have to say, when I saw how strongly and courageously Regina fought back, but by then it was too late.'

The silvery grey man looked unhappily at the pair of them.

'You wretch! You rotter! You miserable worm!' yelled Fizzy, banging her cup down so hard on the table that the chocolate spilt.

Fennymore said nothing. He couldn't even move. It had been almost three years since his parents had disappeared. Three years in which he'd almost got used to his lonely life with Aunt Elsie and Monbijou. And deep down inside, he'd been hoping all the time that his parents would return one day and everything would go back to normal.

'You haven't an ounce of decency,' Fizzy went on. 'To take both of his parents from Fennymore –'

'No, no, not both of his parents,' said the silvery grey man. 'When I realised the doctor had landed me in it, and that no way had Regina been at death's door, I couldn't let Fenibald suffer the same fate. But what could I do? I couldn't let him go back because then the doctor would realise I hadn't kept my part of the bargain. So I modified Fenibald's brain and took him with me. He's here.'

Chapter 12

*In which Fennymore meets his father and finds
out what it means to be brain modified*

The candle on the table had burnt down half way.

It took Fennymore a few moments to make
out the big wing-back armchair in the furthest
corner of the room. Without really knowing what
he was doing, he got up from the table and walked
slowly to the armchair. His legs felt weak, as if
they would stop obeying him at any moment. His
scalp crawled. Did he really want to know who
was sitting there? And if it really was his father,
would Fennymore recognise him?

What had he looked like? Fennymore tried to
remember. Everything was blurry. A big, smiling
form in the Invention Capsule. Short dark hair. A
gentle voice. That was all.

Fennymore had reached the corner by now
and he was standing quite close to the armchair.

There really was someone sitting in it. A man. He sat bolt upright, his hands resting on his legs. His head was bowed, as if he was sunk right into himself. His dark hair was streaked with white. His beard was grey and shaggy. Fennymore was close enough to touch him.

Then the man whispered something to himself. 'Rootle, tootle,' he said.

Or at least that was what Fennymore heard.

'Rootle tootle, hairy foot. Square root, what a hoot.'

Fennymore raised his left hand and touched the man on the shoulder. Very lightly. Far off, as if through cotton-wool, Fennymore could hear Monbijou snorting. Then the man lifted his head slowly and looked at Fennymore. Or rather he looked through him.

'Square root, what a hoot,' he repeated almost inaudibly.

The man seemed not to notice Fennymore, although he was standing right in front of him. Tears sprang to Fennymore's eyes, and at the same time he was overwhelmed by anger. With Aunt Elsie, who had gone and died on him. With Monbijou, who had brought them to this place. And with the silvery grey man.

He looked more closely at the man in the armchair. There were deep grooves in his face, or in the parts of his face that weren't covered by his beard. His gaze was fixed. This was supposed to be his father? No way.

Fizzy came over from the table and looked curiously at the man in the chair. He went on staring aimlessly into mid-air and moved his lips soundlessly.

'Good afternoon, Herr Teabreak,' Fizzy said. 'I hear you are the father of Fennymore here.' She poked Fennymore in the ribs. 'So, well, I'm Fizzy.'

The man didn't seem to have taken in what Fizzy said. Only his whispering got a bit louder.

'Rootle tootle, teabreak root. Teabreak, me break, tea-two-toe.' Then he sighed, sank his chin onto his chest and a moment later a soft snoring filled the silvery grey man's hut.

Fizzy turned around and raised her eyebrows.

'Well, you've made a right mess of this,' she said to the silvery grey man.

Unable to move, Fennymore stood all the time with his back to the table. This man was not his father. He couldn't possibly be. His father had never had such a long beard. And if it *was* him … Fennymore didn't dare to finish the thought.

Then a bony hand was laid on Fennymore's shoulder. Fennymore swung around.

'He'll come right,' said the silvery grey man. 'Every day for the past three years I've given him a herbal potion to keep the brain modification active. If he doesn't have the potion any more, then the effects will recede and he'll be right as rain in a week or two.'

'It's all the same to me,' said Fennymore, brushing the silvery grey man's fingers away. 'You're mistaken. That's not my father.'

The silvery grey man looked sadly at Fennymore. 'It is, Fennymore. Three years ago, just after your mother –'

'Oh, good!' cried Fizzy far too loudly. 'There's still some hot chocolate left. Who'd like some?' she asked with exaggerated cheerfulness.

The silvery grey man gave a little cough and said nothing.

'Rootle tootle,' whispered the man in his sleep.

Fennymore looked at the hands resting quietly on the trouser-legs. They didn't look as old as his face. He'd often watched his father working deftly on an invention. Had it been those same hands?

He suddenly knew what had to be done.

'We'll take him with us,' he said decisively. 'We'll take him back to The Bronx. First thing in the morning.'

Suddenly everyone was talking at the same time. Monbijou gave an excited neigh. The silvery grey man let out a stream of prevarications, and Fizzy could be heard saying 'Wonderful' every now and again.

When it went quiet in the hut, Fennymore said seriously, 'We know now that Dr Hourgood wanted to get my parents out of the way.'

The silvery grey man gave the floor an embarrassed look, nodded and almost blushed.

'But what we don't know …' Fennymore went on, and paused dramatically. 'What we don't know is why. And to find out, we have to go back. And you …' He pointed at the silvery grey man. 'You are going to help us.'

Then Fennymore looked at the long-haired man sleeping in the armchair with his chin on his chest. 'And if that really is my father, it will perhaps be good for him to be in a familiar place.'

As they settled down to sleep on a pile of blankets in a corner, Fizzy cleared her throat loudly and said distinctly, 'I just have one teeny-weeny question.' She turned to the silvery grey man and asked, 'You're not Death, by any chance, are you?'

'My name is Hubert,' said the silvery grey man, giving his head a sheepish scratch.

Chapter 13

In which the very same company sets off on the return journey to The Bronx

Fennymore was woken the next morning by some kind of racket.

'Stop!' he shouted to the silvery grey man. 'Running away is not allowed.'

Hubert was feeling his bony knee and cursing. He almost smiled when he looked at Fennymore's angry face.

'Fennymore,' he said, 'I know you have a very poor opinion of me, but …'

'Poor doesn't come anywhere near it,' said Fizzy in disgust. The noise had woken her up. 'Lousy, shabby, miserable, mean.'

The silvery grey man raised his hands. In his right hand he held his long thin wooden cane. 'I'm not going anywhere, children,' he announced.

'I'm coming home. After all, I have work to do. It's been a long night.' Then he gave a hearty yawn.

'Huh,' said Fizzy. 'And we're supposed to believe you?'

'Take a look at Fenibald,' he said. 'He hasn't had any of his potion since yesterday evening. Maybe abstinence has had some effect.'

'Potion, lotion, what a notion,' came from the big wing-back armchair.

Fennymore looked closely at the man who was still sitting in his armchair in the farthest corner of the room. In the bright light of morning it seemed even more unlikely that it was his father. But why would the silvery grey man try to palm some crazy stranger off on him? Fennymore couldn't think of a reason. But this hair and this beard? No. Or maybe yes?

'Eh, hello, Dad,' he tried.

'Sad lad,' said the bearded man with a giggle.

He was still looking right through Fennymore, but there was something in his laugh that seemed vaguely familiar to Fennymore.

Then Monbijou came right up to the armchair and snorted and nuzzled the bearded man on the knee. The man stretched out his hand and laid it on Monbijou's handlebars.

'Ah,' he said. 'Gah.'

Fizzy put her head on one side and said, 'For sure.' She looked at the bearded man with wide-awake eyes. 'How are we going to get him to The Bronx?'

***

Monbijou hardly knew what was going on. He waited impatiently until they had sat Fennymore's father – or rather Beardy, as Fennymore had privately christened him – on the back carrier, which took all their strength, and had tied him tightly to Fennymore. Fizzy climbed up on Monbijou's handlebars.

'I'll be along as soon as I have washed up the cups,' said Hubert. 'I'm three times faster than Monbijou anyway.'

Fizzy wagged her finger at him. 'We'll see you at The Bronx, and woe betide you if we don't.'

'He'll come,' said Fennymore.

And then Monbijou raced off. A little more carefully than the last time, when they'd travelled through the night, but fast enough all the same that they jolted along and everyone needed to hang on to each other good and tight.

'Oops-a-daisy, we're all crazy,' cried Beardy, his long hair blowing in the wind.

Fizzy tittered. 'I don't know, Fennymore,' she called back over her shoulder. 'I never met your father before, but I kind of like him.'

'Father, rather, all a blather,' chuckled Beardy from the carrier.

Fennymore didn't know what to say to Fizzy. It was all very well for her.

Even Monbijou seemed to think that this Beardy was his father. But he was so different. And even if he *was* Fennymore's father, and even if the effects of the potion wore off in a week or two – who was to say that he would be the same as before?

Monbijou leapt over a particularly large pothole, and two long arms crept around Fennymore from behind. Beardy leant his head against Fennymore and his beard prickled his son's back slightly through his shirt. Fennymore got a warm feeling in his tummy.

They rode on over fields and meadows, through rain and sunshine, past countless big and little rainbows that were lodged in trees and grasses. When the sun was high in the sky they came to the haystack where Fizzy and Fennymore had rested on the outward journey. They reached the little stone wall early in the afternoon. Just as on the day they had left, it had only stopped raining and everything was sparkling in the sunshine. Behind the wall stood The Bronx against the blue sky.

'We're here!' cried Fizzy and jumped down from the handlebars in one leap.

When everyone had dismounted, Beardy stood there astonished, with his mouth open. He blinked at the sky and looked back in the direction from which they had come, over the fields and out into the wide blue yonder. Then he noticed the little stone wall and took a deep breath.

'Ah!' he said again. 'Gah.'

They climbed over the wall, stepped through the garden gate and at last they were outside The Bronx.

'Home!' said Fennymore, looking at Beardy. Would he recognise it?

Beardy was looking around him with interest. Fennymore followed his gaze. The front door was wide open.

Chapter 14

*In which Hubert makes himself important
and an utterly uninvited guest appears*

Somebody had been kicking up a storm in The Bronx. The pots of herbs that were normally on the window sill lay shattered on the floor. Somebody had lifted the carpet and thrown it back down carelessly on the floor. Even the big sofa was upside down, its four wooden legs sticking helplessly in the air. A corner of the multicoloured comfy blanket was sticking out from under it.

Fizzy's eyebrows shot up in surprise as she looked around. Fennymore gulped. Somebody had been looking for something. But for what? He didn't own anything valuable, apart, perhaps, from the silver cutlery he had used on Sundays when Aunt Elsie came to lunch, but that was lying untouched on the table. Although one of the two gold-rimmed china plates lay in pieces on the floor.

He looked at Beardy, who was standing in the doorway looking sort of lost. *If only Dad were back to normal!* thought Fennymore. If indeed he *was* his father.

Beardy gazed with interest at the untidy room but gave no sign that he recognised it. He giggled softly.

'Hey,' said Fizzy quietly, looking at Fennymore. 'It looks just like your great-aunt's place. When we moved in, everything was in a mess, just like this. The furniture had been thrown around and even the nightdresses with all the flowers on had been yanked out of the drawers.'

Suddenly the air shimmered and Hubert materialised. Fizzy stopped talking and gave him a puzzled look. The silvery grey gentleman gave a little cough and, as everyone stared at him, he patted down his silvery grey coat with an elegant gesture. Then he tossed a few wisps of hay aside with the toe of his silvery grey shoe and looked around him.

'Now I know why I live such a Spartan life,' he said. 'All that tidying up is a terrible nuisance. Ah, I see that Fenibald has become acclimatised. How is he?'

But Fennymore didn't answer. It had all become too much for him. Apparently it had looked just like this at Aunt Elsie's also? The last time he'd been there, everything had been the way it had always been. What could all this mean?

Then something occurred to him, something very important. He rushed past Hubert and Fenibald, who was bleating, 'Hubert, honey-pie.' In the hallway, he slipped on the rag rug and went sailing into the kitchen, his arms flailing.

The drawers of the old kitchen cabinet had been pulled out and the contents lay scattered on the floor – multicoloured rubber bands, the little paper flags that Fennymore always stuck in his banana-splits, dried-out conkers from last autumn and all kinds of knives, forks and coloured plastic ice-cream spoons. Even the oven was open and there were wisps of hay everywhere. Only the old waste-bin was exactly as Fennymore had left it. The lid was closed and there were no banana skins or pâté wrappings lying near it. Fennymore's heart pounded. He took off the lid and looked inside.

Under a vanilla ice-cream tub lurked the corner of the tea-towel in which Fennymore had wrapped the vinegar-chocolate tin. Relief spread through him. Encouraged, he reached into the bin and pulled out the chocolate tin. A pungent smell reached his nostrils.

Fennymore unwrapped the tin quickly, threw the tea-towel back in the bin and banged it closed. Done! But then he saw something – something that should not be in his kitchen. The polished toes of two shoes were jutting out from behind the bin, pointing right at him. The left toe was tapping impatiently up and down.

'Harrumph,' went a deep voice.

Fennymore looked up and into the face of Dr Hourgood. Two little light-blue eyes smouldered under his bushy eyebrows. But there was no sign of the jolly doctor face that Fennymore was familiar with. There was something cold about the look the doctor gave him.

'Well done, my dear Fennymore,' said the doctor with pointed politeness, 'for opening that bucket for me. That will spare my calf-skin gloves.'

He looked around, wrinkling his nose, and gently stroked his hands, which were encased in cream-coloured gloves. Then he stretched them out towards Fennymore.

Fennymore clutched the chocolate tin desperately and stared at the doctor with his lips tightly pressed together.

'Well, well, well,' said the doctor. 'I didn't come all this way for nothing.'

A fat gloved hand shot out and made a grab for the chocolate tin. 'Hand that over, if you please.'

At that moment, Fennymore woke out of a daze.

He turned on his heel and started to run out of the kitchen, but the door was closed. He rattled the door handle, but it was useless. Locked.

Dr Hourgood gave a soft laugh. 'You haven't a chance against me,' he said quietly. 'It would be best if you just gave me the tin.'

Fennymore looked around wildly. The window over the sink – would he make it? But he had no time to think. He took a leap and landed with one foot in the washing-up basin. *Crrrrrack!* The dishes. He almost lost his balance, but then he yanked the old wooden window open and, with the box clamped under his chin, he jumped down onto the soft lawn.

As soon as he had pulled himself together, Fennymore gave the two-finger sausage dog whistle as loudly as he could. Hopefully Monbi-jou and the others would hear him and realise he was in danger.

Chapter 15

In which Fennymore tries to read a message

Fennymore had made it safely onto the roof of The Bronx. He was still gasping for air. It hadn't been easy to get up here with the tin in one hand. Why hadn't the others come to his help? Had they not heard his whistle?

At least he had saved Aunt Elsie's chocolate tin. It was lying next to him on the buckled roofing felt. He rubbed his finger over its tin surface. Where he'd rubbed the dirt away, the lime-green colour of the tin and the logo of the vinegar-chocolate company appeared. Why on earth was Dr Hourgood so keen to get hold of this tin?

Then Fennymore heard the creak of the front door from below him. He lay on his tummy on the warm roof and peeked down over the edge. Dr Hourgood was coming out of the door. Fennymore could see the dome of his belly billowing out under his black hat. The doctor was carrying a sack over his shoulder. Fennymore recognised it. It was Monbijou's hay-sack, but there was clearly no hay in it now – it was too stuffed for that. Fennymore squinted and tried to see more. The sack didn't seem to be heavy. At least, Dr Hourgood had no problem carrying it.

He was standing right under Fennymore now. He looked all around, to the right and to the left. Fennymore wriggled back, but the doctor didn't look up at all. With swift and confident steps he was making hotfoot for a car, which was parked behind some bushes. It was a big shiny black vehicle, far too big for the little dirt track that led to The Bronx. The sunflowers, which normally reached up towards the sky here, had been pushed aside, and the car had completely mangled some of them.

The doctor dropped the sack into his car boot and closed the lid. Then he got into the car, his cream gloves gleaming on the black steering wheel. A huge cloud of dust rose up as the doctor accelerated. And then he was gone.

Fennymore climbed down off the roof. The doctor had left all the doors open, and Fennymore strolled through the hall into the living room. It was empty.

'Monbijou?' asked Fennymore. 'Fizzy? Hubert?'

But there wasn't so much as a glimmer of sky blue, not the tiniest freckle and not the smallest scrap of silvery grey fabric was to be seen.

On the table lay a piece of paper. Someone had written something on it in ink. Fennymore had seen this ink before. Dr Hourgood's fountain pen! He picked up the piece of paper and held it right in front of his nose. Oh, these letters! He couldn't make head or tail of them. It was pointless. Fennymore looked around the room once more. Was there really nobody there?

He stuck his fingers in his mouth again and whistled the sausage dog signal.

A terrible snoring came from the sofa, which was now standing the right way up. The comfy blanket, which was spread out over what looked like a little mountain, moved, and a tangled white head of hair appeared from under it.

'Wah!' yawned Beardy, raising his arm in a stretch and staring at Fennymore in surprise.

Oh, no, thought Fennymore with a guilty pang. *I'd almost forgotten about him.*

Beardy was starting to seem a bit more like his father. Something about the look in his eyes.

'Er, hello, Dad,' he said again tentatively.

Beardy said nothing, just looked at Fennymore.

'Tell me, you wouldn't happen to know where the others are?' Fennymore asked.

Not that he expected to get a sensible answer. But he didn't know what else to say.

'Hubertwork,' said Beardy, sitting up.

Fennymore started. That was the first time Beardy hadn't spoken in rhyme. Could the effects of the potion be fading already?

But his hope was short-lived.

'Snip, snap, shiver, quiver,' cried Beardy.

Then he gave a little cluck and started to giggle. He giggled and giggled until he fell back on the sofa and rolled with laughter on the blanket.

Here we go again, thought Fennymore.

He took another look at the note from Dr Hourgood. At the same moment, Beardy caught hold of it, still giggling and snorting, 'Shiver quiver.' He gave a tug and there was a tearing sound and Fennymore was left with only a scrap of paper in his hand.

'Stop! What are you at?'

But Beardy didn't stop. With obvious enjoyment, he started chewing on the paper.

'Stop it!' shouted Fennymore frantically. How was he going to bring Beardy to his senses? Before long the paper wasn't going to be decipherable at all, regardless of whether Fennymore could read or not.

He thought suddenly of the sponge that he still had in his pocket. He pulled it out and offered it to his father.

'Look. A sponge. It's definitely nicer than that paper.'

Beardy backtracked and looked at the sponge.

'Ah,' he said. 'Gah.'

He stretched out both hands and let the paper fall.

Fennymore picked it up and tried to smooth it out. The ink had blotted in a couple of spots and Beardy's saliva had made it go soggy in places.

'That's just great,' said Fennymore with a sigh.

Beardy was busy with the sponge. He was turning it over in his hands and sniffing at it.

Fennymore took a deep breath. He was going to have to try. He knew a few letters anyway. The ones in his name, for example. There, just next to a spittle stain, was an F, just like at the start of Fennymore. And then there was an i. He knew that one because it looked so jolly with that dot on top. Not half bad. And then came a z. He knew that one, it was the last letter of the alphabet because it was so zig-zaggy. Then another z and then … what letter was that? Oh, yes, it was a y. There was one of those in his name too. So it said … F-I-Z-Z-Y. Fizzy!

Fennymore's stomach gave a lurch. What had Fizzy to do with the doctor? He was going to have to read more. Better start at the beginning.

It took Fennymore ages to more or less decipher what Dr Hourgood had written on the piece of paper. Some of the letters had gone blurry and were very difficult to make out. Others he'd never seen before.

Beardy had fallen asleep over his sponge and Fennymore was able to concentrate in peace on what he could read of the letter.

I'_ _ _o_ Fizzy. I_ _ou wa_ _ _o rescue he_, brin_ _he _in. _his e_en_ _.

Fennymore couldn't read the end of the letter at all because it was missing. His father must have eaten it. The page was extremely damp there and a piece was missing. The last legible thing was –*asse*. At the very bottom were a few letters with dots between them.

Fizzy and *rescue* were the only complete words that Fennymore could read. Rescue. *Rescue?* Suddenly it all fell into place. The sack! Dr Hourgood had kidnapped Fizzy. She'd been in that sack! Oh, why on earth hadn't he realised sooner? He might have been able to do something about it. But it was too late now. His eyes flew over the letters and he tried once more to understand what the letter said. *his een*. It made no sense. *wao rescue.*

Beardy wasn't much help either. Fennymore doubted if he would be able to read in his present condition. And besides, he really didn't want to take the risk that the letter might be half-eaten again.

No. There was only one person who could help him. 'If you feel lonely in the next few weeks or want to talk to someone, you're welcome to call round any time.' That's what Herr Muckenthaler had told him, as they said goodbye after that weird visit they'd paid to Aunt Elsie's flat. And now he urgently needed someone to talk to.

Fennymore shook Beardy's shoulder carefully.

'Wake up, Dad. And you're going to have to behave yourself now.'

Chapter 16

*In which Fennymore and Beardy take
a bus and get a few strange looks*

The bus stop was a rusty pole with a battered
yellow sign on top. It was just there on the side of
the road, and Fennymore and Beardy stood beside
it. Beardy rubbed the pole and piously examined
the rust that came away on his fingers.

'Stop that,' said Fennymore and pulled him
away from the pole. He was jumpy. When on earth
was this bus going to come? He hadn't a clue about
the timetable. And how was Fizzy doing? Fennymore poked a few coins out of his little purse.
Hopefully it would be enough.

It rained. Then it stopped. Then it rained again.
And then the bus came.

Fennymore heard it coming a long way off. It
sounded different from the cars, which zoomed
quietly past him and his father and didn't stop.

Oh well, thought Fennymore. *Would I have stopped?*

Beardy was jumping up and down all the time in a puddle that had formed near the bus stop, his hair streaming in the wind. That made the mud splatter, and he laughed loudly and joyfully the whole time.

The engine droned and there was a rumbling sound as the bus lurched to a halt in front of Fennymore and his father. The doors hissed open. Beardy was taken aback. He stared open-mouthed at the big yellow vehicle. Fennymore turned the coins over in his hand and hesitated.

'Will you be ready any time soon?' asked the driver impatiently. 'Are you coming or aren't you?'

He was wearing a blue hat with the logo of the bus company on it. His face looked out from under it, not friendly, but not unfriendly either.

Fennymore took Beardy by the hand. As soon as they had climbed on board, the driver pressed a button and the doors snapped shut. Beardy was astonished into silence and stared at the driver. The bus driver glared back, appalled. For the first time Fennymore realised how mad Beardy looked, with his mud-streaked wet clothes and his long hair.

He quickly pressed Herr Muckenthaler's piece of paper and the coins into the driver's hand.

'What's all this about?' said the driver crossly. 'Number six, Lerchenweg. I'm not a taxi. I can take you as far as Taubengasse. It's five minutes from there. And make sure this fellow doesn't create any trouble,' he added, looking at Beardy.

'Er, yes, of course, thank you,' said Fennymore softly.

The bus was half-full and the passengers craned their necks curiously. Fennymore dragged his father, who could hardly take his eyes off the driver, down the bus. One man who was sitting by the window moved pointedly onto the aisle seat. Fennymore pushed his father onto a free seat further back, and the driver pulled off.

Beardy was enthralled. He gave little cries of delight as the world flew past and banged on the window with his fist.

'Now, now,' called the driver and gave Fenny-more warning looks in the rear-view mirror.

The two ladies who were sitting in front of them were whispering excitedly. Fennymore could make out an 'impossible', an 'irresponsible' and a hissed 'And as for that brat'.

The lady by the window was wearing a hat with a little yellow feather in it. Oh no, thought Fennymore, but it was too late. His father had also seen the feather and had just given it a hefty yank.

'Hee-hee,' he said and tickled the other lady on the neck with it.

Fennymore blushed to the very tip of his left ear.

'So sorry,' he said quietly.

But the ladies sat there stonily and didn't even turn around. Could they be afraid?

Fennymore had to laugh. He took the feather carefully out of his father's hand and stuck it back in the hat.

'No,' he explained to Beardy, 'that is not your feather.'

Then he pointed at the trees and clouds that were going past outside.

Beardy listened with interest. Then he said 'Ah. Gah.'

Wonderful. He'd planned to think about Dr Hourgood and Fizzy's kidnapping on the journey and also about how he was going to explain the whole thing to Herr Muckenthaler. And instead he was having to report the names of trees and to search for clouds that looked like animals.

But Beardy liked it. He hung on Fennymore's words and looked with interest out of the window.

Soon the first houses of the town came into view. A neon sign for the Tristesse Ice-Cream Parlour flew by. Then the bus stopped and the driver called out behind impatiently, 'So, what's the story? Taubengasse.' Fennymore stuck the vinegar-chocolate tin under his arm, pulled Beardy hastily and stumbled, under the disapproving eye of the driver, out into the drizzle.

'Layabouts. Corner-boys. Scoundrels.'

He could hear the voices of the two ladies ranting and raving.

Then the doors of the bus closed again with a hiss.

Chapter 17

In which Fennymore finally opens the vinegar-chocolate tin and Herr Muckenthaler has an idea

Herr Muckenthaler lived in a little flat-roofed house whose front garden was scented with mint and basil. He had looked a little surprised to find Fennymore and Beardy outside his house. His hair was a bit messy and he looked as if he'd just been having a little snooze.

'Fennymore,' he said. 'How are you? Come in.'

'Em, hello,' said Fennymore. 'This is probably my father.' He pointed at Beardy.

Herr Muckenthaler looked at Beardy.

'But he has been brain modified,' Fennymore added. 'That means he's a bit odd.'

Beardy looked back seriously at Herr Muckenthaler.

'Hm,' he said. 'Take off your shoes and come on in.'

Beardy's shoes were caked with mud. Fennymore opened his laces and helped him out of the shoes. Woollen socks striped in red and white came into view. Or rather what was left of what had once been red and white striped socks. They consisted mostly of holes and they gave off an absolutely indescribable stench. Fennymore's stomach heaved. He held his breath and gave an apologetic look in Herr Muckenthaler's direction, but he'd already disappeared.

When Fennymore, holding his father's hand, entered his teacher's sitting-room, Herr Muckenthaler came into the room from a little kitchen nook carrying two large cups of coffee and a dish. He put everything on a low table.

'That's all I could find quickly,' he said, looking apologetically at Fennymore's father. 'A few old bits of peanut brittle.'

But Fennymore's father was totally engrossed in the shelves that were piled up to the ceiling with books and records.

'Ah,' he said. 'Gah.'

Fennymore didn't feel the least bit hungry. He was far too agitated for that. But he sat down all the same beside his teacher on one of the cushions that were scattered around the table. He wanted to show him the note from Dr Hourgood right there and then, but he suddenly got another terrible twinge of conscience about missing school. And anyway, he really didn't know where to begin.

So he tried some of the weird little things in the dish, which looked like dried-out larvae. They crunched softly and had a kind of musty flavour. The coffee didn't taste all that great either. Frau Plüsch's honey cookies had been decidedly better.

After they'd chewed a bit on the peanut brittle and had half-emptied the coffee mugs, Fennymore was starting to feel a bit fidgety.

Using all kinds of roundabout phrases, which came out of his mouth all twisted up, he thought, he tried to explain to Herr Muckenthaler what had happened. Beardy was standing there the whole time gaping in astonishment at the bookcase.

'And here is Dr Hourgood's message,' Fennymore finished, handing Herr Muckenthaler the piece of paper that he had partially deciphered.

'This is Dr Hourgood's message?' Herr Muckenthaler repeated dully, staring incredulously at the paper. 'Fennymore, you know, what you've just told me is completely unbelievable.'

Fennymore shrugged his shoulders.

'It's not – logical,' added Herr Muckenthaler. He sighed, took a long slug of coffee and stared off into the distance.

'Please read it. Fizzy has been kidnapped and …'

'All right,' said Herr Muckenthaler and held the paper up to his face.

'This is certainly Dr Hourgood's handwriting,' he said, staring at the paper.

Then he gazed seriously at Fennymore. 'Fenny-more, if this is a joke, please tell me now. It's really not funny.'

Fennymore looked at the floor. He could feel tears building up behind his eyes. Funny? No, it was not particularly funny that his father had lost his reason and Fizzy had been kidnapped, Monbijou had disappeared again and Hubert had obviously done a bunk. It definitely wasn't funny.

He cleared his throat but said nothing.

Then Herr Muckenthaler read:

I've got Fizzy. If you want to rescue her, bring the tin. This evening. Uhrengasse.

Dr R. U.

If you want to rescue her. This evening. Uhren-gasse. How come he hadn't been able to work that out for himself? Fennymore's heart beat faster.

'Herr Muckenthaler, we have to go. We have to …'

The teacher gestured towards Beardy, who was standing at the window now, muttering to himself.

'Hourgood. In a hood,' he was saying softly to himself, looking seriously into the garden. 'Seldom good, seldom good,' he muttered on, almost inaudibly, and Fennymore could see a tear glistening on his cheek.

***

It took a while to convince Herr Muckenthaler that they had to do something. He was fascinated by Hubert and the way he would materialise. He kept asking Fennymore to repeat details about how that happened.

'Interesting, most interesting,' he kept murmuring and then he would stand up to look something up in one of the books on the bookshelves. Then he'd give a little nod and stare into the distance. Beardy had that effect on him too. He kept trying to get him to talk. A few times, Beardy had let out something in rhyme, and Herr Muckenthaler had seemed very impressed and had made notes.

'Very interesting, Fennymore. A very special case. He is very intelligent. You can tell from his utterances. Was your father very mathematical?'

Fennymore did eventually manage to get his teacher to concern himself first and foremost with Fizzy and the letter.

'Right then,' Herr Muckenthaler said, slamming his book shut. 'So what's in this tin, then?'

The tin! Fennymore had almost forgotten about the tin. Reluctantly, he handed it over to Herr Muckenthaler. Herr Muckenthaler weighed it in his hand and looked curiously at Fennymore.

'I don't really know,' Fennymore said. 'It all happened so quickly, I didn't have time to open it. I think it's Aunt Elsie's valuables.'

Herr Muckenthaler clicked his tongue and held the tin out to Fennymore. 'You're the one who should open it,' he said. 'After all, it's yours now.'

Fennymore took the tin in both hands. Most of the dust had been rubbed off it by now. Carefully, he placed his thumbs under the lid and pushed it up. In the tin, neatly arranged in rows, were about two dozen vinegar chocolates wrapped in silver foil. So this was Aunt Elsie's valuables? Ancient confectionery?

Fennymore unwrapped one of the sweets. The chocolate had gone mouldy and it smelt of feet. Though that might have been coming from Beardy's socks.

'Urgh,' went Fennymore.

Herr Muckenthaler said nothing.

At least he's not laughing his head off at me, thought Fennymore. *First salt-baked sausage dog and now mummified vinegar chocolates.*

Irritated, he let the tin fall onto the carpet. The dusty spheres went rolling off in every direction, but now Fennymore could see something else. Fennymore reached out quickly for it. Flat and heavy, the thing lay on his palm. A large silver key.

'Excellent,' said Herr Muckenthaler. 'Do you know what it's to?'

Fennymore said nothing. He'd been expecting jewellery, gold coins, gemstones – although, or perhaps because, he had never seen Aunt Elsie with such things – or at the very least an envelope full of money. But a key?

Then he suddenly remembered. His father, with short hair, making his way through the currant and gooseberry bushes and past the compost heap right to the very end of the garden. To the Invention Capsule. He was taking a large key out of his pocket and opening the padlock. Then he gave Fennymore a friendly slap on the back and told him to go and play in the sunshine. But Fennymore wanted to go in and watch his father. To invent something himself.

And then, a few weeks after the day his parents had disappeared, Aunt Elsie making that same journey, running through the fruit bushes, ignoring the thorns. Twigs were smacking Fennymore in the face. She stopped at the door of the Invention Capsule, breathing hard. Then she drew the key out of the padlock and held it up in the sunlight.

'You're never to go in here again, Fennymore,' she said. 'You must promise me that. And I'll get rid of the key to this horrible hut. All this invention nonsense has brought nothing but trouble.'

'I remember now,' said Fennymore, and then he told Herr Muckenthaler the whole story.

After that they sat for a while, saying nothing and looking at Beardy, who was taking a little snooze on the carpet, using a pile of books as a pillow.

Then Herr Muckenthaler suddenly said, 'I have an idea.'

Chapter 18

In which Fizzy has to cope with Dr Hourgood and an unpleasant cat

Fizzy opened one eye carefully. She could make out the blurred outlines of the furniture. A massive writing desk, a set of armchairs, a glass cabinet full of things. Where was she? Her body felt like lead and she had a horribly dry mouth.

Wearily, she closed her eye again and tried to remember. Nothing. She tried opening the eye again. Everything was still all blurred. But there, in front of her, something was moving in one of the armchairs.

'Miaow,' went the something in such a piercing voice that Fizzy opened both eyes with the shock of it and saw an orange cat in front of her, watching her out of narrow yellow eyes.

The creature was fat. Unbelievably fat. Its fur gleamed. It looked as if it was brushed for at least two hours a day.

'Wah,' went Fizzy in disgust. She sank back further into her squashy armchair. She hated cats.

'Miaow, miaow, miaow,' went the cat again, this time a full tone higher.

Fizzy put her hands over her ears.

On the third miaow, the door opened and Dr Hourgood came into the room. He had a plate in his hand, and there was a sudden smell of fish.

'Hmm,' he said.

The cat stretched its orange-striped tail stiffly in the air and moved the tip of it back and forth, purring all the time.

Fizzy nearly got sick from the smell of fish. And then the sight of this doctor, who had Fennymore's parents on his conscience, just waltzing in here as if nothing had happened.

He picked up the cat, stroked its fur gently and sank, cat in arms, into the armchair. He held out the plate to the cat.

Creamed herring, thought Fizzy. Disgusting!

'So, Merle,' said Dr Hourgood to the monstrous animal, which had immediately started to chew voraciously. 'You've done a good job of keeping watch.'

The animal gulped the fish greedily, burped and then rubbed itself against the doctor's legs.

Fizzy stared at his hand, which was still stroking the orange fur. It was wearing a cream-coloured glove.

And then it all came back to her. She'd been in the living room in The Bronx. Fennymore had just run into the kitchen. Hubert's wand had begun to vibrate. He'd said, 'Oops! Work!' and dematerialised. Fizzy had put a blanket over the sleeping Fenibald and looked around the devastated room. And then there'd suddenly been this sweet smell of almonds and a hand in a cream glove had pressed a cloth over her mouth and nose.

'You creep,' she snarled now at Dr Hourgood.

The tender look disappeared from his face as if someone had turned it off.

'Miss Kobaldini,' he said in a tone that Fizzy knew well. It was the tone the supermarket cashier used when her mother had to put the bill on the tab again; the tone of the official at the social-housing office when she said, 'The houses have been otherwise allocated to respectable, taxpaying citizens.'

And Fizzy knew exactly how to respond to this tone. She gave the doctor a dignified look.

'Correct,' she said, with marked politeness. 'And whom have I the pleasure of addressing?'

Dr Hourgood looked at her for a moment, at a loss for words. Then he twirled his moustache and said, 'Most amusing. I see that the desperate financial situation of your clan is out of step with your manners. All the better. It'll be easier to put in the hours until evening.'

Fizzy felt like jumping up angrily, but then the cat stood up, arched her back and farted.

'It's all right,' said Dr Hourgood, looking menacingly at Fizzy. 'It's all right, Merle.' He stroked the cat's enormous back. 'Our guest knows what's what.'

Fizzy gave the cat a wary look. Not only was the creature fat, but it had incredibly sharp teeth. She'd better change tack.

'Could I please have a glass of orange juice?' she asked politely. 'I'm terribly thirsty. And I have a headache.'

The doctor laughed mirthlessly. 'Of course. The chloroform,' he said quietly to himself. But then he did actually get up, go to the glass cabinet and pour Fizzy a drink.

She took a quick look around the room. There were heavy striped curtains at the windows. Everything was big and expensive looking – the light-blue armchairs, the table, the sideboard, on which stood an enormous crystal bowl full of fruit. The cabinet was almost hidden by Dr Hourgood's body, but Fizzy could see that it contained bottles and lots of silver trophies.

The doctor noticed her looking.

'All awards from the city,' he said, and his already enormous body swelled even more with pride. 'Chairman of the Union of Business People, mayor for life, honorary doctorate, Executive Chairman of the Council of Rain-Hat Retailers and' – he paused dramatically – 'Honorary Member of the Sports Association.'

Fizzy gave a snort. The cat looked threatening and laid back its ears.

Dr Hourgood cleared his throat, handed her the glass and went on talking.

'And there'll be another honour to add to those shortly,' he whispered meaningfully, and his light eyes became even lighter for a moment. 'An honour that is far more important than any of the others. One that will ensure that the name of Dr Rufus

Hourgood will forever be enshrined in the chronicles of the city.'

Ooh, I'm dying to know, thought Fizzy, gulping down the cool juice greedily. *Honorary Chairman of the Association of Owners of Fat Cats?*

'So, this evening, my endeavours of the last three years will finally be rewarded. It was a bitter disappointment that I found nothing in the flat of Elisabeth Grosskornschroth ... but now it's all starting to come right. Your little friend will come ambling in here and hand over the necessary information on a plate, all to rescue you, you little brat.'

And then Dr Hourgood laughed so hard that his belly wobbled up and down. The cat gave him a horrified look for a moment, but then noticed Fizzy's face and nestled dutifully against its master.

'Well, I have things to do. And so that you won't be bored in my blue salon' – he gave Fizzy a meaningful look – 'I have something for you. Merle likes this very much. Don't you?'

And with that he handed her a large silver brush.

Chapter 19

*In which Fenibald Teabreak puts a carefully
thought-out plan into action*

Boris Muckenthaler had just said goodbye to
Fennymore in the twilight in his front garden and
now he took a deep breath. He went back into his
house and shut the door. It smelt a bit musty. That
must be because of his guest's socks.

It was an unbelievable story that his pupil had
just served up to him. But he had the feeling that
he had to take it seriously. Very seriously indeed.
It wasn't just the bold handwriting of the doctor
on the ransom note, but the story of the silvery
grey gentleman had perplexed him. Fennymore
had said that he'd seen him on the threshold of his
great-aunt's flat. And at the very moment Boris
Muckenthaler had remembered quite clearly that
he'd had a weird feeling, as if someone had stuffed

a lump of pistachio ice-cream down his collar and it had run slowly down his back.

And then there was Beardy. Herr Teabreak. Herr Muckenthaler had never met Herr Teabreak before, but he had to admit that there was a certain resemblance between Fennymore and Beardy – as far as you could tell, considering the man's crazy beard and long hair. In any case, he wasn't just some vagabond. And this story about the invention. That made him very curious.

Herr Muckenthaler went back into his living room. Beardy had woken up and was just eating a potted plant.

'No!' cried Herr Muckenthaler and wrenched the pot from him, but there wasn't much left of the plant. 'Oh dear, of course you're hungry.' He made an embarrassed face. 'Please excuse my lack of hospitality. Unfortunately the peanut brittle is finished, but I'll make you a cheese sandwich right away. You'll have to eat it on the way, though. We haven't got much time.'

That was because the plan he'd hatched demanded great precision from everyone involved. And this was how it went. While Fennymore was making his way to Dr Hourgood's villa at Uhrengasse 83 with the chocolate tin and its contents –

twenty-four dust-encrusted vinegar chocolates and a large silver key – in order to ransom Fizzy, he, Boris Muckenthaler, was to deliver Fennymore's father into the custody of Frau Plüsch and then he had to go to The Bronx and find Fennymore's father's invention.

As soon as Fennymore saw the key, he'd realised that Dr Hourgood must be after the invention. He had described the day before his eighth birthday to Boris Muckenthaler. How his father had told him about the invention with which his parents were going to change the world. And how the two of them had disappeared the following day. And then the break-ins at Aunt Elsie's and at The Bronx. It all made perfect sense.

Boris Muckenthaler did not have to think for long. He'd thought immediately of the key of his own pantry, which looked remarkably like the key from the chocolate tin. So they'd simply swapped the keys.

Dr Hourgood would surely go straight to The Bronx with the key. He and Fennymore were in agreement on that. And by the time Dr Hourgood discovered that the key didn't fit anywhere, he, Boris Muckenthaler, had to be back at Frau Plüsch's. There they'd all meet up and together they would ring the police, so that they could catch Dr Hourgood red-handed. Because otherwise the police just wouldn't believe them.

Fenibald Teabreak munched on his cheese sandwich and made no objections to having his shoes put on.

'Gouda, Cheddar, cheesy feet,' he crowed, a few crumbs of cheese falling out of his mouth.

'So, Herr Teabreak,' said Herr Muckenthaler, holding his breath. He put his cord jacket on and put one of his rain hats on his guest's head. 'Let's go.'

It had got dark by now, but the sky was clear and there wasn't as much as a tiny cloud to be seen.

'Ah,' said Fenibald, looking up at the stars. 'Gah.'

'Now, this is the plan …' said Boris Muckenthaler as they set off, and he started to outline the next steps. He was sure that Beardy, although he appeared to be quite mad just at the moment, basically understood every word. '… and just as Dr Hourgood is searching the house –'

'Aaaargh!' screeched Fennymore's father so loudly that Herr Muckenthaler's heart almost stopped.

He looked at Beardy, horrified. He had gone totally white, had balled his hands into fists and was staring at a big black car that was driving along the street.

Boris Muckenthaler recognised the vehicle. 'Oh, dear,' he said. 'The doctor's car. We really must hurry now, before ...'

Chapter 20

In which Monbijou reappears

Monbijou slowed down and tried not to squeak so much. Why had he been so uncooperative when Fennymore had tried to oil his chain recently? A little bit of quiet would not be a bad thing right now. He cycled slowly over the cobblestones on Uhrengasse, trying to read the house numbers.

'49, 53 ...'

Not at all easy. Several of the villas had no numbers at all, or they were so overgrown with ivy that he could hardly make them out.

'75, 89 ...'

It couldn't be much further now.

A car came driving by. The headlights threw bright stripes of light over the dark street and Monbijou pressed himself, as well as he could, against the wall of the nearest house. He sank right into the ivy undergrowth. Please don't let anybody discover him!

As luck would have it, the car drove by. Monbijou reappeared, freeing himself from ivy tendrils. He'd rather have had hay. He thought nostalgically of the delicious pile of hay that still lay untouched in the kitchen of The Bronx.

But he was on a mission. He absolutely had to help Fizzy out and speak to this cat. What a piece of luck that he had met her on the day that Aunt Elsie had died. Although he was in a pretty dicey situation just now, he almost giggled when he thought about it.

After Fennymore had disappeared into the house that day with his teacher and the neighbour, Monbijou had followed the doctor and his fat orange-striped cat. He didn't quite know why. He'd just had this feeling.

It had happened a few houses along. The doctor had knelt down on the footpath and shovelled a little heap of something into a plastic bag. He'd groaned as he worked, because he'd had to bend his stomach so much. The little heap stank horribly and obviously belonged to the cat on the lead, who was waiting half a metre away, purring.

Then the doctor had suddenly cursed and pulled off one of his cream gloves with a disgusted look.

'Oh, Merle,' he'd wailed. 'Now look what you've gone and done to my lovely glove.'

The cat didn't take the slightest bit of notice. As far as she was concerned, the doctor had got himself and his glove into this mess all by himself. Ranting, the doctor had stuck the glove along with the stinky stuff into the plastic bag.

'Don't ever do that again,' he ordered, shaking the plastic bag. 'Never do that again, or I'll tell Hubert to do the same to you as he did to Fennymore Teabreak's parents. And you know, I have him eating out of my hand.'

The cat had given a startled miaow and rubbed herself against the doctor's legs. Then she'd made herself as small as she could – as small as it was possible to be, considering her size – had lain down on the pavement and looked up at the doctor.

'Get up, you stupid beast,' he'd yelled, yanking on the lead. 'Otherwise I'm going to have to shampoo you again.'

Then the cat had seen Monbijou and had let out three loud, blood-curdling miaows one after another. The doctor had reacted immediately. He'd stretched his hand out, quick as lightning, towards Monbijou, shouting, 'Spy! Bugging device! I'll show you!'

But before the doctor's big hand could get hold of him, Monbijou had scooted away with a squeal of his tyres. He'd heard enough. Now he knew for sure what he'd suspected all along. The silvery grey man, whose hideaway he had discovered years previously on one of his forays out into the wide blue yonder, had something to do with the disappearance of Regina and Fenibald Teabreak.

He'd gone immediately to the hut under the elm trees. Of course, the silvery grey man had not wanted to admit anything, and that was why he'd had to go and get Fennymore. It had been a stroke of luck to find Fennymore and Fizzy by that delicious haystack.

So then, when Dr Hourgood had shown up in The Bronx and just taken Fizzy away, he knew immediately that he had to free her. And maybe he'd be able to get hold of the fat cat and prise some more information out of her.

Suddenly he heard something. Footsteps. He hid quickly behind a neatly trimmed yew bush beside Dr Hourgood's house. The footsteps came nearer and shuffled up the porch steps. Then the doorbell rang inside the house.

Who could be paying a visit so late? Curiously, Monbijou peered out between the leaves. Fennymore was standing outside the door, a tin under his arm. He was rocking back and forth nervously.

Before Monbijou could do anything, the door opened and the enormous form of Dr Hourgood appeared. Monbijou went quickly into reverse and went around the corner into the doctor's garden. And what he saw there made him give a little leap of joy. The patio door was slightly ajar. The last thing that Monbijou heard before he slipped carefully into the house was the deep voice of the doctor.

'Harrumph, it's about time,' he was saying to Fennymore. 'Come in.'

And then the front door closed.

Chapter 21

In which Dr Hourgood breaks his promise

'Harrumph, it's about time,' the doctor said, looking at the tin. 'Come in.'

Fennymore entered the house and the front door closed behind him.

Just keep calm, he said to himself.

But that was easier said than done, three centimetres from the man who had arranged his mother's disappearance and was responsible for his father's madness. He noticed the heat and the smell of peppermint that the doctor's body gave out and he shuddered.

He must just keep nice and calm and polite, as discussed with Herr Muckenthaler. Otherwise the doctor would smell a rat and that would be the end of the plan.

The doctor gave Fennymore an amused look. 'I told you, you haven't a hope against me.'

Fennymore swallowed. He was boiling with rage and he had to make an effort to control himself and not kick the doctor on the shin. They were still standing in the entrance hallway of the villa. There were doors in all directions and an ornate staircase, carpeted in red velvet, led up to the first floor.

'Well?' said the doctor, stretching out his hand.

Fennymore handed over the tin obediently. He felt like a right idiot.

'Ha!' crowed the doctor triumphantly as he raised the lid and peered inside.

'Eh, what's in it, then?' asked Fennymore, trying to look as innocent as possible.

The doctor gave his moustache a thoughtful tug.

'And where is Fizzy?' asked Fennymore. 'Can she come with me now?'

'Odd,' murmured the doctor thoughtfully. 'I expected the mechanism. Or at least a construction blueprint. But this ...' Carefully, he set the chocolates aside and held the key up to the light. 'This changes things, obviously.'

The pale, cold eyes of Dr Hourgood became colder than ever and his face took on an extremely eerie, decisive expression. And then Fennymore felt himself being shoved hard in the back and was suddenly in complete darkness. Behind him, he heard the sound of a key being turned in a lock.

'You must understand,' came a muffled voice, as if through a door, 'that I have to check it all out. If this key takes me to where I want to go, then I'll let you and your little friend go.'

And then Fennymore heard a noise, followed by a 'Harrumph' and the sound of the front door closing.

Chapter 22

In which a fat orange-striped cat changes her mind

It was dark and smelt of peppermints. Another smell also invaded Fennymore's nostrils. A medicinal kind of smell that seemed somehow familiar. Fennymore felt around in front of him. There was some kind of bed or couch, covered in a smooth material. And here? He banged against something hard and a few utensils clattered to the floor. He must be in the doctor's consulting room. He'd been here with his mother that time he'd had tonsillitis. Unfortunately he couldn't remember much about it. But he could taste again the horrible medicine on his tongue. He spat in disgust.

He thought to himself that Dr Hourgood didn't have a decent bone in his body. Anyone who could make such an appalling pact with the silvery grey man wouldn't think twice about breaking a promise to an eleven-year-old boy.

Then Fennymore heard a lot of clanking and banging and the door was pushed open. Monbijou was standing there, ringing his bell excitedly.

'How did you get here?' Fennymore cried, grabbing hold of his old blue bike delightedly by the handlebars. 'Come on, quick. We have to find Fizzy. The doctor has her locked up here somewhere.'

They opened every door that led off the swanky hall. Nothing. Or at least no Fizzy. The rooms were full of expensive furniture and paintings. In one room there were shelves full of gleaming silver cups, and in the last room they looked in part of Aunt Elsie's goods and chattels had been piled up. Fennymore recognised cushions with birds on them, old chests and a sofa with a yellow throw. It was all tied up with Aunt Elsie's green washing line and, right at the very bottom, a flowery nightdress poked out.

Fennymore had seen enough. Panting with rage, he banged the door closed and looked around the hall. Monbijou turned hesitantly towards the stairs. Then he gave a lurch and started to clatter up the red carpeted staircase, leaving a trail of dust and earth behind him. It would serve Hourgood right, Fennymore thought gleefully, racing up the stairs behind Monbijou, two steps at a time.

They could hear it even through the door. A loud combination of purring, hissing and indignant mewing. Fennymore rapidly unlocked the door. Luckily the doctor had been so sure of himself that he'd left the key in the lock.

Fizzy was sitting in a pale-blue velvet armchair, holding a large silver brush in her hand. Her face was scratched and she was

grimacing disgustedly. Lying in front of her on another armchair was an oversized orange cat, and every time Fizzy stopped brushing, it smacked her with its paw and gave an awful squall.

Fennymore would have nearly died laughing at the expression on Fizzy's face, only that she was so horribly scratched.

'Fennymore, at last!' Fizzy cried, flinging the brush in a wide arc across the room and falling on his neck.

The cat pulled itself up with a snarl, arched its back and was just about to leap onto Fizzy's back with its claws unsheathed, but Monbijou was too quick for it. He caught it in a headlock between his frame and his front wheel and rang his bell loudly.

Fennymore took a step back, dismayed at Fizzy's sudden display of emotion.

'Heavens, Fizzy, that needs disinfecting.'

'I'm bloody well going to get cat-rot!' She spat in disgust on the carpet. 'I had to groom that cat all afternoon. And I hate cats. What kept you so long, Fennymore?'

He filled Fizzy in quickly on all that had happened. Monbijou still had the cat in a headlock and was ringing his bell at it all the time. The cat mewed back. It sounded almost like a conversation.

Suddenly Monbijou let the creature go.

'Are you mad, Monbijou!' cried Fizzy. 'She needs to be locked up. For at least a hundred and fifty years. On bread and water.'

But the cat looked innocently at Fizzy and Fennymore and purred. Then she scuttled over to Fennymore and rubbed herself against his legs. Fizzy took a startled step backwards as the cat approached. The cat backed off and then lay down on the floor and looked ingratiatingly at Fizzy.

'I think she wants to stay with us,' said Fennymore, and when he saw Fizzy's expression, he couldn't help himself. He burst out laughing.

Chapter 23

*In which a lot happens at once and two
stinky socks play a decisive role*

'And Hubert really hasn't turned up again?' Fizzy
yelled into the wind. 'The miserable wretch.'

She was holding onto Fennymore for dear
life on the back carrier as Monbijou raced as fast
as he could along the main street towards The
Bronx.

They had decided to change the plan and not
to wait for Herr Muckenthaler at Frau Plüsch's.

'Ring the police?' Fizzy had cried in horror,
when Fennymore told her the plan. 'Fennymore,
you can't seriously think they would arrest him. He
is the mayor and probably an honorary member of
the Commissioner-in-Chief's bowling club.' And
so they had decided to bring Dr Hourgood to
book all by themselves.

'Miaow,' came from the basket that was hanging on the handlebars.

'She must be hungry,' said Fennymore. 'What does a cat like to eat?'

'That one eats creamed herring,' Fizzy announced in disgust.

Fennymore's tummy rumbled. No wonder. Herr Muckenthaler's stale peanut brittle was definitely not what you would call nutritious. He longed for a banana-split. He must have said the word out loud, because Fizzy answered him immediately. 'What? Banana-split?'

Fennymore recited a piece out of the *Dictionary of Inventions* into the wind.

Banana-split: A sundae with bananas, cream, vanilla ice-cream and chocolate sauce. Was invented more than a hundred years ago in the USA. Peel one banana per person, halve it lengthwise and lay it on a plate. If there is a crack in the plate, the banana will do a super job of hiding it. Add a spoon of whipped cream and a scoop of vanilla ice-cream. For the chocolate sauce, simply melt half a bar of chocolate in a saucepan and pour over. Enjoy.

Fizzy was just about to ask what on earth 'Enjoy' meant, but they'd just arrived at the little dirt track that led straight to The Bronx's front door. Monbijou slowed down.

'Right, quiet please. Concentrate,' whispered Fennymore. 'We have to get this right.'

***

Fennymore's father was moving through the wood. He didn't know exactly who he was or what he was doing here, but he had the distinct impression that he had to do this. That car – he suddenly felt sure that was what the big shiny thing was called – had triggered something in him. Looking neither right nor left, he set off cross country. A few times something wet fell from the sky and he got cold, but he kept running further and further and then he saw it in the distance – a large house looming up blackly against the dark grey sky. He was in the right place here – he could sense it. Carefully he came closer. The words 'house' and 'Bronx' formed in his head.

And there it was again, the dreadful car. It was parked directly in front of the house. He wanted to kick it, trash it. But no, better to keep quiet.

Boris Muckenthaler came panting to a stop behind him. 'Herr Teabreak, that was at least five kilometres. You are in admirable condition.'

He came forward, holding his sides. Then he also noticed the doctor's car.

'He's here already,' he said. 'Herr Teabreak, it's getting dodgy. We'll have to –'

But Herr Muckenthaler didn't get a chance to say what he thought they had to do. Beardy put a finger to his beard and said, 'Pssst.' Then he crouched down, took Herr Muckenthaler by the collar of his cord jacket and dragged him through the gate.

The door to The Bronx was open and a light was burning inside. They could make out the outline of a fat body moving behind the windows. The huge shape moved here and there, bent down and after a while shot up again. He didn't fit in here.

'That wretched brat!' a deep voice cried out.

That voice!

Everything suddenly came together in Fenibald Teabreak. He consisted now of nothing but rage and strength. He let go of Herr Muckenthaler's collar, pulled his shoes off – those were called shoes – and started to creep towards the door in stocking feet.

'Herr Teabreak, I think we'd better –'

Once again, Fennymore's father put a finger to his bearded lips and said, 'Pssst.' Then he said in a firm voice, 'Hourgood, seldom good.'

Herr Muckenthaler suddenly felt limitless admiration for this man who wasn't going to let anything stop him, brain modification or no brain modification. He, Boris Muckenthaler, was going to help him, whatever it took.

The deep voice of the doctor, cursing indignantly to himself, grew louder.

'It can only be in the garden, and if not, woe betide that boy!' it said, and then Dr Hourgood stepped menacingly out of the door.

***

They were almost at the house. Monbijou stopped so that his squeaking wouldn't give them away.

'You'd better take the basket,' Fizzy whispered to Fennymore, looking suspiciously at the cat, who had curled up inside it and was watching them out of half-closed eyes.

They crept carefully closer, past the doctor's car. They could see a beam of light and hear a deep voice calling something out loud.

'That's him, the wretch!' snarled Fizzy.

'Pssst,' went Fennymore. 'Concentrate. On the count of three, we'll all jump on him together. Merle, you are to give him a good scratching on the face. And then we'll have to tie him up good and quick.'

'With the washing line that he pinched from your great-aunt,' said Fizzy with a giggle.

'Pssst,' said Fennymore again. 'Let's go. One –'

They were at the garden gate.

'Two –'

Fizzy went to open the gate and Fennymore gripped the handle of the basket.

'And ...'

Now they could hear the doctor quite clearly.

'Help! What ... umph!'

'... three!'

As one, Fizzy and Fennymore jumped out from behind the gate. What followed was indescribable chaos. Arms, legs, stomachs, heads – and somewhere in the middle of it all, Fennymore. He could just make out a scrap of light brown corduroy. And was that a blue eye, surrounded by freckles, gleaming out from behind a strand of grey hair?

'Help!' yelled Fizzy from behind him. 'What's going on here?'

'Hee-hee! Done and dusted, cress and mustard,' tittered a voice that sounded remarkably like Beardy's.

Fennymore tried to move, but he was stuck fast.

'Take it easy,' came a muffled voice from underneath him. Herr Muckenthaler. 'Fizzy, I think you must be on top. Can you jump down, please?'

The weight on top of Fennymore lifted.

'And now you, Fennymore.'

Fennymore carefully extracted his limbs from the heap and climbed down. By the time Herr Muckenthaler and Beardy had sat up, there was only one person left on the ground. Doctor Hourgood's arms and legs were stretched out a long way and he wasn't moving. He had a red and white striped sock over his mouth and one over his nose. The cat sat next to him, her fur all rumpled, looking accusingly at Fizzy and Fennymore.

'Fennymore!' cried Beardy suddenly. 'My son.'

Fennymore didn't stop to think even for a second but leapt forward and flung his arms around his father, holding him as tight as he could.

Chapter 24

*In which Hubert turns up again and
Dr Hourgood is rendered harmless*

They had made themselves comfortable on the big sofa in the living room. Fenibald had settled his head on his son's shoulder and was snoring quietly. Dr Hourgood was still unconscious. He lay on the carpet, tied up in Aunt Elsie's washing line. His fat cat sat next to him, licking his fingers in their gloves. Evidently she felt sorry for her master after all.

Fizzy stared at the animal with a disgusted expression on her face.

'She was supposed to be on our side?' she asked doubtfully.

Fennymore looked up. He was suddenly in a very good mood. He had his father back, after all.

'Oh, come on,' he said to Fizzy. 'It's kind of nice that she's sticking by him. He's so defenceless all of a sudden.'

Herr Muckenthaler interrupted them. 'Fizzy, I'm going to call Frau Plüsch and ask her to tell your parents that you're safe. It could take a while, though. The phone box is halfway to town. Keep an eye on Dr Hourgood while I'm gone.'

He grabbed his cord jacket and went out into the night.

Herr Muckenthaler had hardly gone out the door when the air shimmered and Hubert materialised in the middle of the room.

Fennymore and Fizzy stared at him.

'Have I missed something?' he asked, seeing their astonished faces.

This time it was Fennymore who found his tongue.

'Missed? Not really. Only that Fizzy was captured and was attacked by an oversized cat, that Dr Hourgood locked me up and ...'

'You've been with Hourgood?' Hubert's voice shook and he shrank back into himself.

Fennymore kept on talking. '... and Monbijou came to the rescue and all the time Herr Muckenthaler and my father were on their way ...' He stopped. 'But this is probably of no particular interest to you. You took good care to dematerialise just before it all started to get tricky. Extraordinary coincidence – don't you think?'

'Yes, a coincidence,' Hubert said lamely.

He looked around the room. He seemed to be still thinking about Dr Hourgood. His hand was trembling. But then his whole long, unbelievably thin body shuddered and he straightened up. 'Of course it was a coincidence. You must believe me. I had things to do. Two old gents from the old folks' home and then also –'

'To tell you the truth, we don't really need to hear the details,' Fizzy interrupted.

Fennymore shivered. He really didn't want to hear any more about Hubert's work than was strictly necessary.

'We just find it rather odd that you had to go to work at precisely the moment when Dr Hourgood turned up,' he said.

'Dr Hourgood turned up here?' cried Hubert in alarm, looking around the room. 'Is he still around?'

Then he finally caught sight of the doctor. For one moment, Hubert's silvery grey face was rigid with dread, but then it relaxed when he noticed the washing line and the red and white striped socks that were still across the doctor's face.

'You devils!' he murmured, deeply impressed, and went walking around the unconscious doctor, wobbling in his weird way as he went. The cat nestled close to her master and mewed quietly.

Every step Hubert took seemed more and more like a skip. His face was beaming. Then he poked the doctor in the side with the tip of his shoe. The cat gave a disdainful hiss but the doctor still didn't budge. Hubert looked totally blissful by now. Just as he raised his other foot, a firm voice warned, 'Hubert!'

The silvery grey man winced. Fennymore's father had woken up and was sitting upright on the sofa with one arm around Fennymore. He was still barefoot with tangled hair and beard, but his eyes had changed. They were clear and bright.

He also felt a lot better. It had come back to him who he was. Fenibald Teabreak, inventor.

'Fenibald,' Hubert replied.

The two men stared silently at each other.

***

It was Fizzy who broke the silence. 'Oh, for good-ness' sake, say something,' she said so loudly that even Dr Hourgood seemed to hear it.

His fat body shook, the socks fell from his face and he opened an eye. His gaze wandered around the room and stopped at Hubert. 'You!' he started in his deep, rumbling voice. 'I'll –'

But Fennymore's father had leapt up from the sofa and pressed the socks back over his mouth and nose. The doctor's body sank back into sleep.

Fennymore looked at the tied-up doctor and thought, *Creep. I'd love to* … But what exactly *would* he love to do?

It seemed he wasn't the only one to be asking this question.

'What'll we do with him?' Fizzy asked. 'Hubert, suppose you … with your wand …?'

Hubert hesitated. The cat mewed so loudly that everyone jammed their hands against their ears.

'No,' said Fennymore quickly. 'I don't want that.'

'So what do you want?' Fizzy snapped, looking at him angrily. 'Maybe you'd like to present him with a cup for barbaric behaviour?'

'What about a little brain modification?' suggested Hubert faintly.

Fennymore's father looked thoughtfully at the doctor, who was lying at his feet.

'Brain modification,' he repeated softly. And then he giggled. Just one little giggle at first and then a louder one, until at last he was holding his sides and snorting with laughter.

'Obviously that's far too amusing a punishment,' said Fizzy.

'I think it's just right,' said Fennymore.

Chapter 25

*In which The Bronx is suddenly swarming with
people and everyone is talking at once again*

It was past midnight.

Monbijou had sloped off to the kitchen to eat
his hay in peace. Fennymore was still sitting next
to his father on the sofa. They just sat there, saying
nothing, his father's arm still around his shoulder. Fenibald couldn't help giving the occasional
giggle and saying something incomprehensible in
rhyme, but most of the time he watched his son
with bright, clear eyes. Fennymore was just happy.

Fizzy had curled up, yawning, on the carpet.

A car door banged outside and suddenly the
night was full of loud voices.

'There they are,' cried Fizzy, jumping up and
running to the front door.

The noise outside was absolutely deafening.
Yells, roars, laughter and, if Fennymore was not

mistaken, there was also a soft barking in the middle of it all.

And then they all came piling into the living room, led by Fizzy's mother, Frau Kobaldini. Fennymore could tell it was Fizzy's mother. She had the same eyes, the same freckles and a pony-tail that was just as shaggy as her daughter's. She put her arms around Fizzy and kept kissing her and saying, 'Fizzy, oh, my Fizzy.'

Then six lads of varying ages came strolling in, looking around with interest. They all had faces full of freckles and they were all wearing brown hoodies. Only the eldest was decked out in some-thing that looked suspiciously like one of Aunt Elsie's flowery nighties. They had to be Marlon, Mustafa, Maarten, Marcello, Moritz and Titus.

Frau Plüsch came tripping along behind Fizzy's brothers, wearing a fur coat over her pink night-dress and with her white sausage dog, Paula, in her arms. Then came a big friendly looking man in overalls. And last of all into the room came Boris Muckenthaler, wearing a big grin on his face.

'Fizzy, oh, Fizzy,' Frau Kobaldini was sighing with tears in her eyes.

'Fizzy, oh, Fizzy.' The boy in the flowery night-dress imitated his mother.

'That's enough, Marlon,' Fizzy's father warned his son.

'May I introduce Mama, Papa, my brothers,' Fizzy called out to Fennymore, grinning all over her face.

'Is that you, Herr Teabreak?' asked Frau Plüsch incredulously, and her sausage dog barked.

And then they all sat down, on the sofa, on the carpet, on the three wobbly chairs that Fizzy's father had brought out of the kitchen.

Fizzy's mother explained hysterically how her daughter had suddenly disappeared and her sons had spent two days turning the town upside down, to no avail, and how they'd all been sick with worry. In the end, Fizzy's father had thought of Elsie Grosskornschroth's great-nephew, and how Fizzy had told him, enviously, that he was in her class but hardly ever went to school. They'd asked Frau Plüsch for the address, Frau Plüsch had ordered a taxi and they had all driven out here together, even though it was the middle of the night. And on the way, they had picked up Herr Muckenthaler, who had been standing outside the telephone box with no change in his pocket.

When they had all told their stories, it had gone quiet, and Fennymore's stomach rumbled in the silence. He looked at Paula, the white sausage dog, and his mouth watered. He tried to think of something else, but he couldn't.

He couldn't ignore it.

He was most dreadfully hungry. Hungry for salt-baked sausage dog. He was desperately hungry for salt-baked sausage dog, even though he always had tummy ache for two days after eating it.

Fizzy's mother gave Fennymore an appraising look and then she clapped her hands.

'Who'd like pancakes?' she asked.

Then everyone started shouting at once.

'But,' said Fennymore diffidently, 'I haven't got any ingredients. I only have ...' He stopped and looked around, embarrassed.

'I thought as much,' said Fizzy's mother. 'That is absolutely no problem.'

Fennymore watched in astonishment as she took a huge carton of eggs, two kilos of flour, a packet of sugar and three litres of milk out of an enormous bag at her feet.

Frau Plüsch was watching her too with undisguised disapproval. 'I wanted to bring honey cookies, but this person here insisted on packing everything but the kitchen sink.'

Fizzy was just about to make a nasty response, but her father gave her a stern look and then turned to Frau Plüsch.

'My dear neighbour, we have been meaning all along to invite you to have pancakes with us. Consider this a special invitation to an out-of-house midnight feast. And of course we have something also for your charming little friend.'

And with that he took a piece of salami out of his breast-pocket. Frau Plüsch accepted the heel of salami and looked around uncertainly. Marlon, Mustafa, Maarten, Marcello, Moritz and Titus grinned.

Paula, Frau Plüsch's green-eyed white sausage dog, chomped with gusto on the salami. Frau Plüsch's features relaxed and she smiled at Herr Kobaldini.

Promising smells and hisses were coming from the kitchen and everyone was chattering away madly all at once. A mountain of pancakes appeared on the dining table, reaching nearly up to the ceiling, and everyone set to eating with hearty appetites, singing the praises of Frau Kobaldini's cooking.

Herr Muckenthaler looked up suddenly from his plate and muttered to Fennymore, 'Tell me, where is Hubert? I'd really like to meet him.' He looked hopefully around the room.

'No,' said Fennymore, who was just biting into his fourth pancake. He couldn't get enough of them. (He really must note this recipe in the *Dictionary of Inventions*.) 'He's working.'

A deep voice came from a dark corner of the room. 'Harrumph!' it burbled. 'Hubert Sockbert,' and giggled.

Chapter 26

In which the story comes to a close – with an invention and a rain-shower unlike any there has ever been on the face of the earth

Fennymore and his father were alone at last. After the pancake feast it had started to get bright. Frau Plüsch, the whole Kobaldini family and Herr Muckenthaler had said goodbye. They had put the giggling Dr Hourgood along with his cat on the bus and told the furious driver to put them down at Uhrengasse and the cat would take him home. As he was leaving, Herr Muckenthaler had invited Fennymore's father to his place the following weekend – to an evening with experts, as he put it – and had pressed the key of the Invention Capsule from the chocolate tin into his hand.

'Goodness me, it is my key,' he'd said delightedly, and as soon as the last guest had got into the taxi he'd made straight for the garden.

'Dad,' asked Fennymore, following him, 'how did this brain modification thing feel?'

Fennymore's father stood stock still. 'Actually,' he said, looking up at the sky, in which big fat black clouds were piling up, 'do you know, it was quite good fun.'

'Fun?' Fennymore was aghast. 'But what kind of a punishment is that going to be?'

'A very good one, as you said,' answered Fennymore's father. 'Just imagine how things are going to go tomorrow morning in Dr Hourgood's surgery.'

Fennymore giggled. He'd love to have a bout of tonsillitis so he could see how Dr Hourgood was going to manage at work.

'So, son,' said Fennymore's father in a happy voice, putting his arm around his son's shoulder, 'let's go and get your girthday subprise.'

'Girthday subprise?' Fennymore repeated. His father obviously hadn't completely recovered just yet from his brain modification.

'Fennymore, if I am not very much mistaken – although that is of course quite possible – you have just reached the age of eleven, and I have a subprise for you. Come on.'

He pulled Fennymore along, past the scrubby currant and gooseberry bushes and the compost heap, to the bottom of the garden. Fennymore hadn't been here for three years, since the day Aunt Elsie had forbidden it to him. The Invention Capsule had become so totally engulfed by vines that they could hardly find the door at first. But then a gleam in the foliage indicated where the padlock was. They used an old kitchen knife to free the door of vine tendrils.

The key fitted and the padlock sprang open with a little click and they were soon standing on the wooden floor of the little room. Inside it looked just as Fennymore had remembered. Everything was up in a mad heap. Fennymore's father always said he needed it that way so that he could think logically. And if you were an inventor, you had to be able to think logically. The drawers of the desk were open, tools and materials pouring out of them. The big shelving unit was, as always, stuffed with unfinished commissions. And on top of a pile of old toasters, which provided spare parts for the Mechanical Waiter, lay the *Dictionary of Inventions*. Like all the books, it was a centimetre thick with dust, but Fennymore recognised it immediately. A draught from outside stirred the dust.

'Ugh!' Fennymore and his father spat particles of dust out of their mouths. But as the dust lifted,

Fennymore Teabreak saw something else lying in the middle of the desk.

Fennymore's father pointed at the little object and said, 'There you are. It belongs to you.'

Fennymore came closer. The thing looked a bit like a sleeping bat: a kind of handle with pleated dark material wound around it with little wires and hinges.

'What's that?' he asked, a little disappointed.

This was supposed to be his parents' invention? Didn't look exactly marvellous. He'd expected something a bit more impressive – a flying apparatus maybe or a banana-split machine. Fennymore turned the thing over in his hands. He felt a button under his fingers. Whumph! He leapt back. What he was holding in his hands now hadn't the slightest resemblance to a bat. A kind of fabric roof was stretched out over the end of the rod that Fennymore was now holding in his hand. Maybe it was some kind of flying contraption after all?

Just at that moment, a rumbling kind of sound could be heard outside. The sky was totally clouded over and it had gone dark in the Invention Capsule. Then came a crack of thunder and rain started drumming so loudly on the roof that

Fennymore could hardly hear what his father was saying.

'What did you say?' he yelled.

His father came so close to his ear that his long hair tickled Fennymore. 'Your mother,' his father shouted into his ear. 'She invented it. I'd got stuck and I wanted to give up. Then she had the idea to …' His voice had got hoarse. He gulped and stopped talking. Then he took a step away, looked his son right in the eye and shouted at him: 'It's a Brumella. Go outside and you'll see.'

Outside? It was pouring with rain. Streams of water were running down the window pane and, through the open door, Fennymore could see that huge puddles were forming in front of the Invention Capsule. And he'd left his rain hat in the house. Then his father put an arm around him and said, 'Come on, we'll go together.'

They went out into the rain, but Fennymore didn't get wet! He looked up in astonishment.

Then Fennymore and his father looked at each other and laughed. They stood arm in arm under the Brumella and laughed until the rain stopped. Then they jumped up and down in the puddles until they were both covered in mud and water from head to toe.

And much later, at the end of a long, fun-filled day, Fennymore and his father sat wrapped up in the multicoloured comfy blanket in the living room, with Monbijou, and Fennymore's father told him all about his mother.

And they were happy all the same.

We hope you have enjoyed reading *How to Bake a Sausage Dog*. The following few pages will introduce you to some other books published by Little Island, which you might also like to read.

HOW BILLY BROWN SAVED THE QUEEN
BY ALISON HEALY
ILLUSTRATED BY FINTAN TAITE

What do you do when the Queen is struggling with a knotty maths problem that only you, Billy Brown, can explain? You travel to her palace in the middle of the night and help the nation, of course! In return, the Queen now wants to come and visit – and you can't say no to royalty.

But the Queen's suitcase contains two tiaras, a spare crown, three evening gowns, a silk dress and a pair of green wellingtons – nothing remotely suitable for visiting the bottle bank. Fitting in is tricky when you're so magnificently different.

A right royal riot of a read!

'Clever, quirky and oodles of queenly fun – suffering ducks, one was most amused!'
Alan Nolan

MY SECRET DRAGON
BY DEBBIE THOMAS

Aidan Mooney has the mother of all problems. His mum is part dragon.

He's spent his whole life struggling to keep her hidden from the world. But now, with the help of his super-smart new friend Charlotte, Aidan discovers a much darker secret hiding in the woods …

'A clever blend of realism and fantasy for children who like adventure tales with lashings of humour and heart.' **The Irish Independent**

'A smashing romp. The writing is excellent.' **Celine Kiernan**

'Unforgettable characters and page-turning action.' **ER Murray**

BUMPFIZZLE THE BEST ON PLANET EARTH
BY PATRICIA FORDE
ILLUSTRATED BY ELĪNA BRASLIŅA

Bumpfizzle is on a mysterious
mission to Earth from Planet
Plonk. His Earth family is OK.
Except for the four-legged
brother (Mr Sooty) and The Baby
– which leaks from both ends.
And when he bites his teacher
(to check if humans are edible),
not to mention trying to sacrifice
a goat, things start to go wrong
for Daniel – er – Bumpfizzle.

'So hilarious! Patricia Forde is definitely the high queen of Irish
comedy.' **Eoin Colfer**

ABOUT LITTLE ISLAND

Based in Dublin, Little Island Books has been publishing books for children and teenagers since 2010. It is Ireland's only English-language publisher that publishes exclusively for young people. Little Island specialises in publishing new Irish writers and illustrators, and also has a commitment to publishing books in translation.

LITTLE ISLAND BOOK GUIDES

Our books are stuffed with ideas that children are going to want to discuss with their friends and their adults, at home, at school, in their library or reading group. So we produce materials which will give teachers, librarians, parents and children ideas about using our books in interesting and innovative ways. All our Book Guides can be down-loaded from our website free of charge and may be used freely in all book-friendly places.

www.littleisland.ie/book-guides

ABOUT THE AUTHOR

Kirsten Reinhardt is a German writer of children's books living in Berlin. *How to Bake a Sausage Dog*, her first book, won the Oldenburger prize for children's literature when it was first published in German. It has been translated into French, Spanish and Catalan as well as English. She has since published three other children's books.

ABOUT THE ILLUSTRATOR

David Roberts is an award-winning illustrator from Liverpool. Since 1998 he has collaborated with some of Britain's finest children's authors, including Julia Donaldson, Sally Gardner, Philip Ardagh and Jacqueline Wilson, to produce stunning children's books. He is also the creator of the popular Dirty Bertie books. He has been shortlisted for the Kate Greenaway Medal and was the winner of the Nestlé Children's Book Prize Gold Award.

ABOUT THE TRANSLATOR

Siobhán Parkinson studied English literature and German at Trinity College Dublin and has worked as an editor ever since. She has written more than twenty books, mostly for children, and won numerous awards. Her most recent novel for children is *Miraculous Miranda*. She was Ireland's first Children's Laureate. Siobhán has translated several books from German for Little Island.